ADVANCE PRAISE FOR
OPEN FIRE

"Amber Lough's volatile mix of gunpowder, strength of spirit, and violence conjures a past so casually detailed it's as if the author lived through it herself. This fierce, loving narrative breathes life into the flames of the Russian Revolution and the muddy, bloody horror of a women's shock battalion storming the trenches of World War I. Katya is a heroine to ache for, and her story is a stunning, vibrant glimpse of a rare moment in women's history."

—Elizabeth Wein, author of *Code Name Verity*,
Rose Under Fire, and *The Pearl Thief*

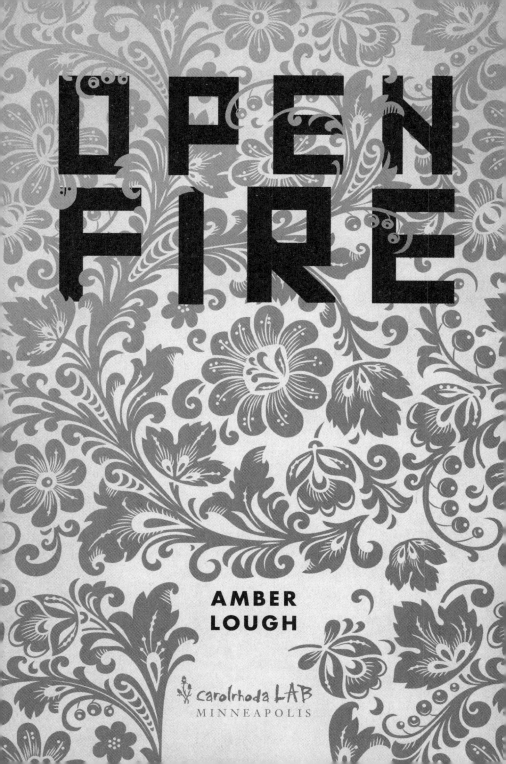

OPEN FIRE

AMBER LOUGH

Carolrhoda LAB

MINNEAPOLIS

Carolrhoda Lab®
An imprint of Lerner Publishing Group, Inc.
241 First Avenue North
Minneapolis, MN 55401 USA

For reading levels and more information, look up this title at
www.lernerbooks.com.

Image credits: FedotovAnatoly/Shutterstock.com (gas mask); penguin_house/
Shutterstock.com (floral print); Bananafish/Shutterstock.com (font);
Rtstudio/Shutterstock.com (texture); Lukasz Szwaj/Shutterstock.com (paper).

Main body text set in Janson Text LT Std.
Typeface provided by Linotype AG.

Library of Congress Cataloging-in-Publication Data

Names: Lough, Amber, author.
Title: Open fire / Amber Lough.
Description: Minneapolis : Carolrhoda Lab, Lerner Publishing Group, [2020] |
    Summary: "In 1917 Russia, seventeen-year-old Katya joins the first all-female
    battalion to fight the Germans, but she soon finds that patriotism alone won't
    help her survive the realities of war" —Provided by publisher.
Identifiers: LCCN 2019006850 | ISBN 9781541572898 (th : alk. paper)
Subjects: LCSH: Soviet Union—History—Revolution, 1917-1921—Juvenile fiction.
    | CYAC: Soviet Union—History—Revolution, 1917-1921—Fiction. | War—
    Fiction. | Soldiers—Fiction. | Sex role—Fiction. | Friendship—Fiction. |
    World War, 1914-1918—Russia—Fiction.
Classification: LCC PZ7.L9237 Ope 2020 | DDC [Fic]—dc23

LC record available at https://lccn.loc.gov/2019006850

Manufactured in the United States of America
1-46576-47593-10/8/2019

FOR MOM AND DAD, FOR GETTING ME THAT *RUSHIN' RUSSIAN* GAME WHEN I WAS ELEVEN AND FOR NOT LAUGHING TOO HARD WHEN I ASKED FOR A YELTSIN DOLL.

PART ONE
RECRUIT

"Everyone admits that the country is swiftly heading for disaster."

—Vladimir Lenin, *Pravda* No. 62; May 20, 1917

"You know already the story of George and the Dragon."

"Everyone knows it, Papa."

"Then let me tell you tonight of Olga."

"I know her too. She's a saint."

"Yes, but that was later. Before, she was the most feared woman of all the Rus."

1

FEBRUARY 23, 1917
PETROGRAD, RUSSIA

THE explosive powder slid into the grenade after a light, quick tap. I dipped the scoop back into the jar, leveled it, and filled the next one on the tray, wriggling my nose to get rid of an itch that had been hovering there for the past seven grenades. The TNT had dyed my fingers a bright canary yellow, and I didn't want them anywhere near my face. I had to forget about my nose.

To distract myself, I mentally recited the characteristics of the grenades while I filled them. M1914 stick grenade. Weight: 580 grams. Length: 235 mm. Filling: 320 grams of TNT. Timing delay: 3.5-4 seconds. Effective range: 15 meters.

Tap, tap, and I filled the scoop with another 320 grams of TNT.

In comparison to the rest of my life, the constant filling of grenades was soothing and predictable, and I rather liked my job. I met my quotas, made sure everyone on my line was safe, and took home a decent paycheck for a seventeen-year-old girl who'd dropped out of university halfway through her first year. Most important, my grenades went to the front and helped Russia fight off the invaders—the Germans and Austrians.

"Pavlova," hissed Darya, the girl to my left. She held her scoop poised over the canister of TNT, but her eyes were on me. "Did you hear about the march?"

I nodded, careful not to move my wrist and scatter the explosive on the table. Everyone in Petrograd had heard about the march. The Tsar had put out a ration on bread, and since the city was already strained by three years of war and a bitter winter, the women were taking to the streets. I didn't blame them, given that the last loaf I'd bought had been gray, not white, and I'd had to wait in line for nearly an hour to get it.

Socialists would probably be there too, calling for rights for workers and the removal of the Tsar. The loudest group of socialists, the Bolsheviks, wanted a revolution. But every time someone tried that, they found themselves either in Siberia or on the end of a rope.

Just the other day, though, I'd found an issue of *Pravda*, the Bolsheviks' illegal newspaper, in one of the bathroom stalls here. Even though I knew it was wrong, I couldn't resist reading it. I'd gobbled each word like it was bitter chocolate.

"Some of us are going after our shift," Darya said, keeping her voice low so as not to distract the other girls on the line.

"To protest the bread rations?" I asked.

She nodded. "My babushka spent all night stitching up a banner. Even she will be there."

I wanted to laugh at the image of an old grandmother sewing letters onto a canvas banner, bickering about the Tsar by the light of a candle. If she was anything like my grandmother, she'd curse the Tsar in one breath and bless him in the next. But Babushka had been gone for six months now, so she'd missed her chance to march in the streets.

I shrugged off the ache her absence always brought. That

was easier to do when I wasn't at home, where her tears still streaked the pane of glass covering her favorite icon. Saint Georgi, of course. "It might be over before we're done here," I said to Darya, "but I'm sure your babushka will tell you all about it."

"It will just be starting when our shift ends. Don't you want to go?"

I hesitated. My father had always supported the Tsar. He had been at the front fighting in the Imperial Army since the war began. And somehow he still found time to write editorial letters to Petrograd's conservative newspapers, defending the Tsar's policies. Although I didn't always agree with my father, I had never stood against him . . . or the Tsar.

"I don't know," I said, keenly aware that it was a coward's answer.

Darya squeezed her scoop till her knuckles bled white. "Each week everything costs more and more but our wages stay the same. If we don't do something about the rations, none of us will have anything to eat by the end of the month. All we can do is protest."

I tapped my scoop hard against the grenade in front of me. I worked because I wanted to help with the war, not just because I needed the money, but I understood her frustration. "We can argue about bread and wages, but our soldiers are dying trying to protect us. We need to stay focused. Make our quotas."

That shut her up.

For the rest of my shift, talk of the women's march slithered along the grenade line, but we didn't slow our pace. Despite the frizzling energy coming off the line, we met all our quotas.

After my shift ended, I went to the washroom, where Masha—my best friend for the past ten years—always waited for me. She would pretend to fix her hair while I scrubbed a layer of skin off my knuckles. The golden tint of the TNT never faded, no matter how much soap I used. It was becoming a routine I strangely appreciated. But today, instead of styling her hair, Masha was waving a rolled-up sheet of paper at me like a baton. The words *Resist the Rations!* blurred before my eyes.

"We have to march, Katya," she said. Her thick, dark braid was pulled over a shoulder and tied with a remnant of war ribbon, frayed at the ends. Despite the worn-out ribbon, Masha glowed with the sort of health that had become increasingly rare as the war raged on. She stood half a head taller than me, as strong and golden-skinned as the fabled Amazons.

"I'm going home," I said, batting the paper out of my face and switching on the faucet.

The water stung like an army of little bees in the cracks and folds of my skin. I grabbed a cake of soap and a yellowed brush and started scrubbing the poison and the cold off the backs of my hands.

Masha tapped the paper on the tip of my nose, right where it'd been itching all afternoon, and I flicked some water at her face. She laughed for a moment before straightening her mouth again.

"Come with me to Nevsky." Nevsky Prospekt, Petrograd's main street, was where everything important happened. If the rumors were true, it would be full of women today, packed in like herring in a tin. "Just for a few minutes, at least. If it's only a handful of college students and a granny or two, we'll pretend we were going shopping. But I want to see it for myself. I don't want to wait for tomorrow's newspapers."

"Mmm." I dried my hands on the sides of my skirt, always the cleanest spot. It was hard to tell if Masha was excited about the women's march itself, or if she was only excited about having something different to talk about.

"Which side are you on?" I asked, taking off my hair kerchief.

"That's not a fair question, and you know it. I'm on the side of not starving to death."

"We'll hardly starve," I pointed out. Her family had enough tinned food to last until Masha had grandchildren. And because my father was an army colonel, my brother and I had access to food stores not publicly available. Besides, we were used to living simply. As children, we'd spent most of our holidays with our father's regiment, mimicking how the soldiers marched, trained, and lived. We would survive this food shortage . . . provided I managed to pay off Maxim's gambling debts soon.

Masha leaned against the sink basin, her gaze roaming across the bathroom to the other girls scrubbing and primping. She didn't have to say anything for me to know she hadn't meant *us*. She meant *them*.

"Idealist," I sighed as I untied my factory apron.

While my father had fed me loyalty and duty with every slice of bread, Masha's parents had buttered theirs with compassion for the common worker.

Masha knew as well as I did that if the bread wasn't rationed, there would be no grain for the men at the front. Her father was fighting too, though he wasn't a career soldier like mine. I massaged the pang in my chest that flared up whenever I thought of my father. I would eat gray bread all winter if it meant they would live.

On the other hand, I knew others were more desperate. It didn't seem fair for the Tsar to tell people to cinch their belts this late in winter, while his own table was as well appointed as ever.

"All right," I said. "Nevsky it is."

We walked arm in arm out of the factory, each of us swinging a lunch pail in a mitten-covered hand. The road to the tram stop was more ice than snow, but we didn't care. Work was done for the day. We were a line of over fifty women, and a song filtered through us, building and growing as it wove its way along. The melody was haunting and sad, and I sang nearly as loudly as Masha, letting the music take with it some of the loneliness I never seemed to shake. Large white fluffs of snow drifted through the air like fairies, and my heart felt warm for the first time in months.

The war would end soon, and my father would come home. It would end in a volley of grenades that I had built. I could feel it in my tingling fingers, no matter what the newspapers claimed.

Once we reached the tram stop, we all split into smaller groups, heading in different directions, and when our tram arrived, Masha and I climbed up and grabbed a handhold by the front. The car was already full of workers who'd gotten in line before us, but we pushed through and found a place to stand. Once we were all aboard, it took off, rattling down the rails to the bridge that would take us over the Neva River and into the center of Petrograd. The car smelled of oiled wood and sweat, and the windows were shut tight against the cold, trapping the scents within. Everyone was talking about the bread rations and the women's march, their sharp voices weaving over and under the benches.

Masha swung on the handle loop like a schoolgirl. "We are definitely going to see this. I wouldn't be able to sleep tonight if I just went on home and pretended nothing was happening."

"It's going to be dark soon," I said, "so I can't stay for long."

She rolled her eyes at me and I let myself swing on my handle, bumping into her.

"Ekaterina Viktorovna Pavlova, are you afraid of the dark?" she gasped in feigned shock, clutching at the glass buttons on her blouse.

"When it's as cold as the Snow Maiden's brittle heart? Yes."

The tram didn't make it all the way to Nevsky Prospekt because the road was flooded with women in long, dark coats. There were men, too, but not nearly as many. It seemed that all the women standing in the long lines at the bakeries had decided to meet in this single spot.

Masha and I climbed out of the tram and made our way in the general direction of Nevsky, holding hands so as not to get separated. A few other factory girls stuck close to us, forming a little pack of lean wolves, skirting the edges of the city's largest flock of woolen coats.

There were placards and banners, chants and songs. I could feel everyone's sense of injustice. The Tsar might be the Father of Russia, but he had been too stern, people chanted. He lived in his glittering palace, with its feasts and parties, and told us to tighten our belts, to buckle down and send more brothers to die in his war.

Some of the women looked as though they'd had to tighten their belts years ago. Their eyes were shadowed by grief for their dead husbands and the long winter of war. The Tsar's cold shoulder had rubbed their pain raw, and they would no longer wait patiently for the comfort of spring. They would drag it out of war's torpid slush by sheer force of will.

I couldn't help but feel the power of so many women, fighting for what they believed in, together. Excitement thrummed in my veins, and although I didn't join them in their chanting, I wanted to be a part of them, to be full of their righteousness.

"I didn't think it would be so big," Masha yelled in my ear.

"Me either!" I shouted back.

"Do you think the Tsar will listen to them?" she asked. Before I could think of an answer, I tripped over a hard ball of slush and lurched sideways into a man.

He caught my elbow, helped me balance, and then grinned in recognition. "Ekaterina Viktorovna?" he asked, and then I knew it wasn't a man, but a student only a year or two older than I. Sergei Grigorev.

We'd had a chemistry class together last year, when I was still studying at the university. We'd shared notes once or twice but hadn't spoken much outside of the class. He'd gotten taller, taller even than Masha, but his hair was the same reddish blonde in a short, clean cut.

"Who's this?" shouted Masha. Her eyes were twinkling, which made me feel oddly nervous.

"Sergei Fyodorovich! You're marching with the women?" I asked. Standing between him and Masha, I felt like a child. I wasn't particularly short, but I wasn't from the same giant stock these two were.

"Of course." He tapped at his shoulder and I noticed the red ribbon tied to his upper arm. "This is the start of a revolution.

Don't you feel it?" His eyes were on fire with something I could barely comprehend. I picked up my pace.

"You're friends with a Bolshevik?" screeched Masha, but she sounded more gleeful than upset. "But you said—"

"We were at university together," I told her, hoping she would hush.

Sergei brushed my sleeve, but his eyes were on the crowd before us. "I was about to head down another street and get to the front. Do you want to come with me?"

I glanced at Masha and the other factory girls, casting about for a polite way to decline.

"Go ahead," Masha said. "I've got my paper girls here to keep me warm." She reached out and put her arm around the shoulders of one of the girls she worked with, and I realized all the girls we'd come with were her friends, not mine.

"You'll get to be a part of the revolution," Sergei said to me, grinning.

"I'm not a Bolshevik," I said, sounding less firm than I meant to.

"Even if you're loyal to the Tsar, you're in favor of letting people eat, right?"

"Of course."

"Then come. See what we're all about." He took my mittened hand and pulled me down an alley full of muddy slush and trash.

I ran to keep pace with him, a mix of anticipation and nervousness pumping in my veins. We made a few turns on some smaller streets until we reached the start of the protest on Nevsky. The crowd marched twenty abreast, forcing onlookers to back up onto the sidewalks and against storefronts, knocking elbows and peering over shoulders.

Nevsky Prospekt was awash in color. The white of fresh snow, the black and navy blue of late-winter coats, the kaleidoscope of scarves, and the bright, bright red of hundreds of armbands and banners. I drank it in, feeling the city's heartbeat thawing in the icy street.

Sergei's cheeks were pinked by the cold. "It's happening. It's actually happening."

Socialists walked alongside grandmothers, mothers, and schoolgirls, carrying banners and signs all in red. The crowd was chanting, "Free the people! Free the workers! Free the bread!"

Sergei chanted with the crowd. With a quick prayer that my father would never know, I joined him. My throat was soon raw from shouting. Everyone around us was cheering, smiling, and so very sure that a revolution was underway. We were *alive* with it.

Then the street began to rumble beneath our feet. Something was coming, and we barely had time to look before a regiment of Cossacks on horseback burst from the intersecting road. They pulled their horses to a halt and filled the street, blocking our way. The horses' coats steamed as they jangled harnesses and stomped their hooves.

Cossacks, with their stiff wool cloaks and gray furry hats, were the fiercest riders in the Imperial Army, riding across the Steppes before they could walk. At the sight of them, the chanting died to a low hum. The heated breath of thousands of protesters rose wispy and white in the February air.

"End this march and go home!" the Cossack leader shouted to the crowd. "The Tsar won't let anyone starve!"

"Tell that to my boy at the front!" someone jeered.

"The Tsar's been starving us for years," another voice cried out.

The Cossack raised an open hand at us, his fingers rigid. "You have no right to protest here! If you do not leave, I will break this march apart through force."

When no one moved, he shook his head as though disappointed. Then he lowered his hand, slid his saber free of the scabbard, and pointed it at the front of the crowd. "Ready!"

Forty or so rifle barrels pointed at us and the crowd shifted like a school of fish sensing a predator.

"Aim!" *Click, click, click.* Rippling down the line, the Cossacks pulled back the bolts and filled their chambers.

Some people scurried away, falling upon one another in the grimy slush. But many of us stood still, our feet rooted in the snow. This couldn't be happening. Surely the soldiers wouldn't shoot these people. They were only women asking the Tsar for bread.

The soldiers were aiming at the crowd. At Sergei. At me.

My heart was beating its way into my throat, and all I could hear was the pulsing of blood in my ears. I could not move. I couldn't even twitch. This wasn't my march, but I was here. I had shouted with the others because I believed in what they were asking for.

Sergei squeezed my mitten and whispered, "They won't shoot with so many women here."

There was a pause—a holding of breath—as everyone prayed the Cossacks would not shoot.

The commander's nostrils flared, and my entire body froze in fear. I was afraid that if I breathed, I'd shatter the world.

"Go back to the Steppes, you Romanov hounds!" A rock whooshed over my head and hit the commander in the shoulder. It tumbled to the ground, the sound muted by the snow.

"Fire!"

An explosive sound tore through the air. Bodies slammed onto the street, while other people stumbled back and slid to their knees. Shrieks of fear, pain, and disbelief ricocheted off the rifles.

Sergei pulled me to his side. For a moment my muscles gave way and I fell into him. I wanted to run, I wanted to disappear, I wanted to go home. But I was not hit. I pulled myself up straight.

The Cossack leader pulled a glove off his hand and wiped at his forehead before shouting a word I could not hear.

The men lowered their rifles, spun their horses around, and urged them into a trot. Moments later, they were gone.

A man barely five meters away was lying in a bright circle of blood that matched the red ribbon pinned to his lapel. Like a soul released, steam rose from the blood surrounding him.

There was a patch of dark stubble on the dead man's cheek. Maybe he'd been excited about the protest that morning and his hands had shaken as he shaved. Now he sprawled out on Nevsky Prospekt, never to shave again.

"They retreated!" Sergei said. "They shot at us, but we won."

We didn't win, I wanted to say to him. *They shot at us, fellow Russians, and we fell.*

"Why were people afraid of a woman, Papa?"

"Men are always afraid of women who have power. Queens, for example, are more frightening than kings."

"Are you afraid of queens?"

"Not all, no. But I would have been terrified of Olga."

2

"**YOU** stood your ground against those Cossacks. You were as brave as the men," said Sergei. His eyes roamed over the street, over the fallen. "They have paid the price for freedom."

I hadn't been brave. I had been frozen in fear. If one of those rifles had been aimed at my chest, I would have died because I'd been too petrified to run. My heart pumped with the sludge of a coward.

Briefly I wondered where Masha had gone. She'd been so far back from the attack, she had to have been safe, and hopefully she hadn't seen anything. She was resourceful and with friends. She'd make her way home without any problems.

Sergei tugged me out of the middle of the street and beneath the awning of a bookstore. He tried to push the door open, but it was locked. "Let's get farther away before the Tsar makes them come back."

"He's not here," I said numbly we turned off Nevsky Prospekt onto the nearest side street. I shuffled in the slush, careful not to slip.

"Who isn't here?" he asked.

"The Tsar," I said. "He's not in Petrograd right now. He's at the front, near Riga."

Sergei slowed, but I kept going, my body shaking with adrenaline. I crossed my arms and stuffed my mittens into my armpits to try to quell the shaking, but there was nothing I could do for the twisting in my gut or the image of the dead man imprinted in my mind.

"How do you know this?" Sergei demanded.

"I overheard it." We'd reached the narrow footbridge that crossed the Griboyedov Canal. The stones were slick, despite the salt someone had sprinkled, but I didn't bother grabbing the railing.

"You don't just overhear the Tsar's location, you know," he said, taking hold of my elbow. I didn't shake him off like I usually would when a man offered me help I didn't need. His touch grounded me, pulled me away from the dead man and back to the bridge. "That doesn't happen."

"It does when you meet with a group of officer's wives once a week on your father's orders. They all like to show off their secrets. Such as how the grand duchesses and Alexei Nikolayevich have the measles at the moment." That discussion had been full of concern, especially for the Tsar's young son.

Sergei's eyes glinted with interest. "I knew there was more to you than was obvious at first glance."

I wasn't sure what to make of that. "I need to go home."

"I'll escort you. Who knows what sorts of people are on the streets right now?"

I thought of the man lying in the snow and how his body steamed from the holes in his coat. He had died in front of me. I wasn't afraid of anyone I might meet on the walk home, but I did not want to carry that image alone. "All right."

The trolley service had been canceled because of the protests, so we arrived nearly an hour later, our boots soaked through and our noses as red as those socialist armbands. Sergei had tried to buoy my mood with talk of the golden future that was sure to come after the revolution. Once the Tsar abdicated and a socialist government took power, Russia's troubles would end. We'd all have what we needed, he said with conviction, and no one would be sponging their wealth off the backs of the poor. There would be equality and justice, for man and woman alike.

His words were cream and berries on my tongue. But as sweet as the ideas were, I knew a revolution would be tart, biting back.

"The Tsar won't willingly give up his power," I said. "And his supporters will resist change every step of the way."

"Yes, but there are more of us than there are of them."

I ignored the expectant look he gave me. If he was hoping I'd volunteer my own loyalties, he would have to cope with disappointment. Did I want the Tsar to abdicate? I wanted him to listen to his people. To do more for those in need. But I also wanted Russia to win the war, and I doubted unrest on the home front would make that easier.

The army private at the entrance to my apartment building gave me an odd look when I brought Sergei in, but he didn't stop us. I had been worried he wouldn't let a socialist follow me upstairs, but Sergei smirked and mumbled something about "revolution in the ranks, too."

"It's on the third floor," I said as we headed up the steps, leaving wet prints on the marble tile. "Our housekeeper has the day off, and my brother has been home all day, so please forgive any mess," I added half-jokingly. My heart kept pace with my feet, each beat reminding me that I was bringing a man to my home for the first time. My brother, Maxim, would be there of course, so there was no reason for this nervous cant of my body.

"You should see the state of *my* rooms," he said with a laugh.

Sergei had always set my nerves on edge. It had been difficult to focus on chemistry with him in the class. I was drawn to his bright eyes, the way he tilted his head, his gregarious laugh whenever he made a mistake. When I left the university for the factory, I'd attributed those feelings to a chemical that must have been accidentally released in the classroom. A loose jar of poison, perhaps, or a gas leak. Now that he was climbing the stairs beside me, I had to acknowledge it was Sergei who had made me ridiculous.

I turned the key in the door, pushed it open, and found the umbrella holder tipped on its side, the ceramic latticework cracked and scattered like icing on a ransacked cake.

"Do you have a dog?" asked Sergei.

"No." I dropped to my knees and searched through the sky-blue bits of ceramic and the umbrellas, all in various stages of wear. It wasn't there. "No pets." My voice was surprisingly calm. "He took it all."

Sergei joined me on the floor. "A favorite parasol?"

"A little leather bag. I hid it in here so my brother wouldn't see it. He never uses an umbrella."

He scooped up the umbrellas and leaned them against the wall. "And the leather bag had something in it?"

"My savings. All of it." Three months' wages, gone. It'd been stupid of me to leave the bag there, thinking it was safely hidden. I'd chosen the spot because I could dispose of the money before going farther into the apartment, but in the back of my mind, I'd known it was risky.

Instead of asking me why my brother would have stolen from me, or why I felt the need to hide my money from him in the first place, Sergei started gathering the shards of the umbrella holder into his hat.

"Do you want me to stay until he comes back?"

I shook my head. "He won't hurt me. It's just that when it comes to money, he can't help himself. It's as though someone else steps into his skin and takes him off to the card tables. He thinks he'll win it all back, all that he's spent, but he never does. Then he comes home, the real Maxim, and he's angry at himself. Not at me." I wiped at my stinging eyes.

We both reached for the same piece of ceramic, and our fingers brushed. "Doesn't your father have his army wages sent here?"

"He does, when they come in. Sometimes the pay's late, and sometimes it just doesn't come. I think my father has been taking less money because of the war. We've all been trying to do with less, haven't we? And I thought that if I could pay Maxim's debts, the ones he keeps gambling to pay back, he could stop. He could calm down, and finish recovering."

Sergei didn't ask, but he raised an eyebrow.

"He was in a battle last October. He had a torn shoulder, burns and cuts from an explosion, and he couldn't sleep. He still has nightmares." My cheeks warmed, and I wished I hadn't said so much. Then I almost laughed at myself—still protective of a brother who'd taken every ruble I had saved.

Sergei grimaced. "This war is a nightmare. Russia shouldn't have agreed to fight in it."

"We didn't exactly accept a formal invitation." My voice sharpened. "We were invaded by another country!"

"That's what we were told, but it isn't the whole truth," he said.

"And you know this how?"

"Much in the same way you know about the Tsar's whereabouts. I listen to people who talk." He winked, doing his best to diffuse my irritation. It didn't work.

"What's the whole truth, then?" I snapped.

"That's a talk for another night." He set his hat full of ceramic pieces on the hall table. "Unfortunately, I live on Vasilievsky Island, and it's going to be a long walk, so I should get going."

Embarrassment at my rudeness flooded through me. "Wait a moment. I'll get a bowl to put that mess in so you can have your hat back. Would you like some tea, too? To warm up?"

He glanced around at the apartment and his cheeks flushed pink. "I'd better not."

With a nod, I ran to the kitchen, grabbed the first bowl I found and the last bit of cheese, and returned. After pouring out the contents of his hat into the bowl, I gave the hat a good shake and handed it to him with the wrapped-up cheese.

"What's this?"

"A snack. I'm sorry I don't have any bread to go with it, but . . ."

He laughed. "That's why we were out there, wasn't it?"

With a grateful tip of his head, he wrapped his fingers over mine, pressing them gently into the hat brim. "Thank you. And thank you for being there with me today. You were incredible." His fingers were hot on mine, melting any last traces of winter.

"Thank you for walking me home." I stepped back and slipped my fingers out of his.

He pulled open the door but then paused. "I have an idea." He looked out into the stairwell and then back again, his eyes as bright as they had been during the walk home. "There might be a way for you to earn some extra money."

"I already work a full shift at the arms factory."

"Yes, but you . . . know things," he said carefully. "You hear things. About the Tsar, for example. There are people in the city—good people with good intentions—who would like to know these things too. And they would pay for that information. It could be after your shift. Whenever you have time."

Who would possibly want to know the gossip of a bunch of bourgeois officers' wives? "The newspapers?"

"The Bolsheviks." He looked more man than boy then. "If this revolution is going to be effective, we need to know everything that's going on."

I stared at him. If I helped the Bolsheviks, I'd be turning my back on my family's support for the Tsar. The ghosts of my brave, loyal ancestors would haunt me.

But they had not been on the street today. They hadn't seen first-hand the brutal truth of a government that does not know or care for its own people.

"I'll think about it," I said, and I shut the door on him with a soft click.

I made myself drink a cup of tea before stripping out of my dress and draping it over the back of the chair in my bedroom. I wasn't sure I'd ever be able to wear it again without thinking of this day, of the gunfire I'd survived.

Was this what Maxim had felt after a battle? He'd been at

the front for two years before he was wounded severely enough to come home. I couldn't imagine how he'd felt night after night, peeling off his uniform, cleaning his pistol, and just breathing. Maybe there'd never been any relief. Maybe those nightmares he had didn't come from only his last battle, but from of all of them, accumulating like beads on a string. Until it snapped.

My brother was not the same boy I'd grown up with. He had left for the front jaunty and grinning, giving me a salute and a kiss on the cheek before leaping onto the train. He'd promised to bring me home a pointy Kaiser's helm from a German soldier, but when he returned last autumn, his eyes were flat and his smile was gone. There were no kisses and the only promise he made was that he wouldn't lose the game this time.

I was brushing out my hair when I heard the front door open and shut. Quietly, I set the brush on the dressing table and swirled around in my stool, gripping at the dry, peeling wood beneath the seat. It took him a few minutes to reach my room. His long, thin frame filled the doorway, the shadows cast by the lamplight shifting across his face.

Maxim had a certain way of slouching that said both that he was sorry and that there was nothing he could do about it. "You're up late," he said. His voice was coarse, probably from a bottle of vodka burning its way down his throat.

Resentment warred with pity as I looked at him. We'd been so close for so long. With a father in the army and a mother who'd run off when I was eight, we'd relied mostly on each other. But I couldn't count on him for anything now.

Quietly I asked, "How did you find it?"

"The money?" He looked surprised. "I tripped over the umbrella stand, and when I went to clean it up, I found that little bag."

I laughed. "You did a hell of a job cleaning up."

He had the decency to look ashamed. "I got distracted."

"Maxim," I said, fighting to keep my voice steady, "until the war is over and we get everything the army owes Papa, we need every single kopek. The money in that bag was to pay back your loan, which, if you haven't forgotten, must be paid by the end of June."

"I'll find work!" he insisted. "I won't go gamble there anymore. I've been kicked out, anyway."

Thank goodness for small mercies. And yet . . . "You can't work extra jobs. The army will just call you back to the front if you do."

He shook his head sharply. "I can't go back to that. It's over for me." I noticed he was gripping the doorframe as though it was the only thing that could hold him up. "I'll write to Papa and ask him to get me released from my commission. Then I'll find work here and we'll pay it all back. That's what I need, don't you see? I need a project. Something different." His right cheek dimpled, and I wanted to both squeeze him in a hug and impale him with a sharp stick. This was the look that had gotten him out of a lifetime of trouble. "I can write well. Maybe I can write for a newspaper. With Papa's connections . . ."

There were more writers in Petrograd than pigeons, but I held my tongue. I hadn't seen this side of Maxim in a long time. He'd swung so quickly from repentance to optimism that I didn't want to crush his spirits.

"And then you can go back to university, get back to your studies," he added. "You can quit your job at the factory with those peasant girls. You shouldn't have to work. Especially in a place like that."

"I'm not going to quit my job as long as there's a war," I snapped. I couldn't let myself think of the university. Of how even Papa had seemed to approve of my ambitions to become a chemist. Of how it was the closest I'd ever come to making him proud of me.

"So you're not doing it for the money?" His tone took on a mocking edge. "I distinctly remember you saying we need every—"

Impatiently, I cut him off. "Can't someone do something for more than one reason? Does it always have to be this or that? It's a good thing I *don't* work just for the money, because that money is gone. Now, please, I had a long day.'" My voice broke, and I coughed to cover it. "I'm tired."

His face fell. Without another word, he stepped back and shut my door.

I didn't cry.

"Was she a warrior?"

"In a way, yes. She fought for her people, and for her son."

"Like a mama bear."

"Some might say her claws were just as sharp."

3

MARCH 27, 1917

IN the very heart of Petrograd, an unassuming door pressed into the corner of a yellow-stoned building. A small brass plaque marked it as a printing shop, but those who read a specific newspaper knew it as the home of *Pravda*.

Pravda had grown infamous over the past month. In a surprise to everyone, the Women's March had brought the Tsar's government to its knees. With his soldiers unable to stomach firing on the crowds again—and with most soldiers turning coat and joining the protesters—the Tsar's fist could not fall hard upon the city. Just three weeks ago, a wing of the socialist movement had seized power, forcing Tsar Nicholas II to abdicate and forming a provisional government.

My poor father's latest editorial—insisting that we needed the Tsar's leadership to stave off a German invasion, and that the socialists were nothing more than weak-willed terrorists— had fallen on deaf ears when it arrived from the front.

Meanwhile, I'd continued to fill grenades. My brother was still waiting to hear if Papa could get him discharged from the army. We were running out of time to pay his debt, so I'd come here to find the only person who had offered me help.

After checking that no one I knew was lurking out on the street or coming down the Moika Canal, I pulled open the door. The small shop was lined in display cases of card stock and letterpress invitations. A shop girl leaned over a book propped open on a display case while rolling a small bust of Pyotr the Great between her hands like a juggling ball. She glanced at me over silver spectacles.

"Can I help you?" she asked, sounding anything but helpful.

I fidgeted with my hat pin, then decided to keep the hat on. "I'm looking for one of the typesetters."

Pyotr the Great was set aside and the book shut with a snap. "You can write down whatever spelling mistake you found and I'll pass it on to the man."

I took a step closer. "I need to speak with him."

The desperation in my voice must have worked, because her hands settled onto her hips and she jerked her head at the door behind her. "Who is it?"

"Sergei Fyodorovich Grigorev."

Sighing, she lifted a portion of the counter to let me pass through. Then she led me through a series of doors, down a hallway, and into a room as large as a tennis court. A wall of windows faced the street, casting bright afternoon light over a pair of printing presses, each manned by a team of two men. The room vibrated with the cacophonous clanging of metal.

Sergei was leaning on one hand and packing pinhead-sized pieces of type into a metal tray. His hat was turned backwards, and his shirtsleeves were rolled up and tied back with red bands. He was leaner without his thick winter coat. My pulse quickened a little at the sight of him, involuntarily. I would have turned around right there if it hadn't been for my brother.

"Sergei Fyodorovich, there's a girl here to see you," the shop girl called over the noise.

His eyes swept up and widened when they landed on me. "Katya! Why are you here? Is something wrong?"

I hadn't expected him to address me so familiarly. I tried not to show how much it took me aback.

"I've been thinking about your offer." I glanced at the shop girl. He took the hint and guided me to a table that had been pushed against the wall. A battered samovar stood like a queen amongst a court of chipped and mismatched teacups. He chose a stoneware cup and fixed me some tea while I eyed our surroundings. No one was in listening range.

"Where have you been?" he asked. "I've called on you several times, but the army guards at your building always tell me you're out."

"I work a full shift."

"I know, but women aren't allowed to work in the factories at night, and I tried then, too."

I didn't need to answer his prying questions, so I ignored them. "My brother hasn't been able to pay off what he owes his creditors. He tried to make money writing—"

Sergei snorted. "Good luck there."

"At least he made an effort." I sipped the tea, glad to find the samovar had kept it warm. It went down smoothly, ignoring the lump in my throat that had shown up when I decided to help the Bolsheviks. "What would your friends like to know?"

Sergei crossed his arms and smiled warmly. "How do you feel about keeping your ears open at these army wives' meetings?"

"That's it?" It sounded too easy, like I'd just be passing on gossip instead of betraying the secrets of my father's institution.

"There might be a few packages for you to pick up and pass along. Nothing big. Notes, usually. The risk would be negligible for you." He picked up another cup and poured himself some tea, which he swallowed in one gulp. "The pay isn't fantastic, but it's for the good of the people. And it might help you."

"Anything helps."

"That's what I always say."

I left him with plans to meet again in a few days. On my way out of the building, the girl with the bust of Pyotr the Great leaned on her elbows over the display case.

"Don't fall for a revolutionary, girl."

I gave her a little salute. "I won't." As I told Masha over and over, this didn't seem like a good year to fall for anyone or anything.

———

APRIL 15, 1917

I laced up my mother's plum-colored gown with the shell buttons. It made me feel older and sophisticated in a way I never dreamed I'd truly be and was better armor than most things I had in my wardrobe. In this gown, I was a young woman who knew what she was about. I was wittier, prettier, and somehow calmer. This was what I wore when I was keeping an ear open for the Bolsheviks. I refused to think of my mother when I wore it.

Last week I'd worn it to Easter tea with General Yudenich's wife, Elena Stefanovna. I'd been a little too eager with my questions about actions at the front—enough that she asked if I was secretly engaged to a young officer. Before I could think of a response, the other wives jumped in with suggestions, warnings, and knowing smiles. By the time I left, I'd gotten two good bits for Sergei.

Since then, I'd been bringing information to Sergei every few nights on my way home from the factory. I paid off a tiny portion of Maxim's debt, which he had not added to, thank goodness.

And the war raged on.

This afternoon, Maxim escorted me down the block, back to General Yudenich's home. Maxim had cleaned up, and if you didn't lean in too close, you might think the stringent smell came from his aftershave. I'd gotten him out of the house, but now I had to make sure no one noticed his half-drunken state.

General Yudenich lived in an actual house, and when I was younger I used to pretend it was a palace. Now I saw how squished it was between the other houses on the street, more like a library or museum than anything grander. Elena Stefanovna liked it that way. She'd filled every public room with books. Each room held books of a specific language—even the dining room, where all the books were French. We were ushered into the foyer by the butler, and then taken to the sitting room—the English room—to receive pre-dinner drinks and meet the others who'd been invited. Elena Stefanovna gave me a kiss on both cheeks, scanned my dress, and then dismissed me to lavish praises on how strong Maxim had gotten since Christmas, and how he should have come to visit at Easter.

"My dear boy—no, don't look at me like that. You'll always be a boy to me," Elena Stefanovna said. Apparently, she hadn't noticed anything wrong with him. She betrayed no signs of disapproval, like a wrinkling nose or a stare into his slightly bloodshot eyes. She turned to the General. "Remember when he and our Ilya raced their ponies across the parade grounds? *During* a parade?"

We all chuckled, then fell awkwardly silent. I'd only been five years old when the boys ran their ponies through the infantry regiment, but I'd grown up in their cadet-shaped shadows. Whenever someone mentioned Ilya, those memories twisted like briars in my gut. Ilya had patiently answered my questions about military rules, taught me how to march, even showed me how to hold a gun and a saber. He said that if I'd been born a boy, I'd be just as good at soldiering as he and Maxim were. Then he was killed in action on November 9, 1915.

If I'd ever have made a secret engagement with anyone, it would have been with him.

The General, newly retired and looking out of place in a dark suit instead of his uniform, shook Maxim's hand. "I heard from your father that you did well out there. You were wounded and yet you still saved two soldiers. Good man."

Maxim had told me that on the day he was wounded, he had a pebble stuck in his boot. He was crouched down in the trench, sliding it off, when the attack came. He'd had to fight in just one boot, climbing up the ladders with his men and charging across the field, only to be knocked down by the force of a nearby explosion. He'd landed on his back, staring up at the early morning sky, before he remembered he wasn't alone.

He was sent home broken, his ears ringing and his skin poked full of holes. I'd watched his body heal, but his soul was still haunted. The General didn't see this, of course. He only saw a war hero who'd survived a battle.

And then he turned his red nose toward me. "What's this I hear about you working in a munitions factory, Ekaterina

Viktorovna? If you wanted to help with the war, you could have been a nurse, like the grand duchesses." I couldn't tell from his stony expression if he was disturbed or proud to learn of my job, and so I did what I always did in these situations: I told the truth because I couldn't think of a satisfying lie quickly enough.

"I wasn't cut out to be a nurse." I forced myself to look him in the eyes when I said it. "So I'm doing what I can."

His stony face softened. "If only more people were like you, dear."

"Darling, you must tell her the funny story!" Elena Stefanovna cut in.

The General turned to his wife, his brows set into something between confusion and irritation. "Which funny story is that?"

"The one about that woman."

"Ah, yes. Let's save that for dinner, shall we? I want to wait till Lermontov is here."

Lermontov was the man I was supposed to take a message from, and the sound of his name made my pulse jump.

Elena Stefanovna took her husband's arm and led him toward the door. "He is here. He's just gone to have a look for a book." She paused and lowered her voice conspiratorially. "In the German room," she whispered. Then, after giving everyone a bright, prepared smile, she guided us into the dining room.

I was placed in front of the French philosophers bookshelf beside a waspish blond in lavender lace who'd once been an actress. Maxim sat across from me, with the General's wife on his left. When the hawk-nosed Captain Lermontov came in, he was seated on my other side. He gave no sign that he knew he was supposed to hand me something.

Other than Maxim, I was the only person in the room under the age of thirty, and after a day at the factory surrounded by hundreds of young women, it felt deeply nostalgic, like I was having dinner with my extended family. This was how it had been when my father had been home.

We were into the second course—and Maxim had, thankfully, abstained from drink and melancholy thus far—when Elena Stefanovna reminded the General of "that woman."

He wiped his face, took a sip of wine, and then leaned onto the table with both elbows. "I've been waiting all day to tell you this, Lermontov. You will love it." He looked up and down the table. "A woman came to visit Kerensky the other day. Not *that* sort of woman, if you know what I mean." He grinned at his own joke. "She got the approval from the Tsar himself to join the army, and has since been wounded twice in battle. The men respect her. To a point. Anyway, she got Kerensky cornered, and after a few hours, had him—the Minister of War—completely on her side. According to her, we've got the morale problem solved."

"The morale problem?" asked the ex-actress.

"We've been having a bit of difficulty getting the soldiers to stick with it," answered Lermontov. His eyes dipped to the edge of the table, then up to me. "Especially since the new government is planning to allow soldiers to form committees and discuss whether a plan of attack is worth the effort." This last bit he said with a full tongue of scorn. Knowing what I did about his leanings toward socialism, I wasn't sure what was an act and what was not. "Naturally, few think *any* attacks are worth it, and some entire battalions are marching back home."

General Yudenich put down his knife and fork. "I believe it to be the most idiotic idea put forth this century." His voice was edged in steel. "It would undermine both the traditions and the authority of the Officer Corps. How can a man keep his soldiers in line if there are no consequences for those who disobey? It used to be, a lieutenant could use his pistol as backup if his motivational words did not encourage the men to push forward. But now they can have committees, they can run off if they don't like that day's operations." He picked his knife back up and gripped it till his knuckles were white. "Mark my words: an army cannot win a war by committee."

The dinner party guests shifted uncomfortably on their seats until Maxim asked, "How will this woman solve the problem, then?"

At this, the General smiled again. "She's going to shame the deserters and cowards. And you know how she's going to do this?" He looked at me, as if I should offer a guess. He even raised a brow, daring me.

"She's going to fight the Germans with a company of Amazons?" I offered.

Everyone laughed.

"Close, Ekaterina Viktorovna. She's going to train a battalion of normal Russian girls and bring them to the front. To fight."

"As soldiers?" asked the actress, with all the drama of her profession.

"Yes, as soldiers." The General looked directly at me. "She's not the nursing type either, not Sergeant Bochkareva. If she'd been born a man, I think she'd have made her way up the ranks by now. A captain, at the least. Normally, I'd say it was wasted on a woman, but she's been useful."

"Isn't it funny?" asked Elena Stefanovna. "A woman will train a battalion of women—with uniforms and rifles and everything."

"Even," the General said, his eyes twinkling at me, "grenades."

All this time, I'd been sitting in my spot near the French philosophers, trying to figure out how I could get into the German room and find Goethe's *Faust*, and suddenly they were talking of women going to war.

Of course I'd seen the stories of the individual women soldiers in the newspapers, but I'd felt they were beyond me. I was not so brave as to march up to a commander and ask to take my place beside fifty men, and I certainly couldn't pass myself off as a man, as some had done. Perhaps if I'd been a peasant girl, working beside men my entire life, I'd have thought differently, but I'd been nose-deep in textbooks until I started making grenades.

I'd done as much as I could at the factory, and still my father was not as proud of me as the General was of this Bochkareva woman. Papa was proud of Maxim, the soldier son who'd followed in his footsteps. Until this moment, that had never been an option for me. But now, women were going to be soldiers.

"What sort of woman would volunteer for such a thing?" asked the actress.

The General's wife laughed. "Peasants, if they can get anyone to volunteer at all. The poor and the stupid."

"We had a woman in our battalion," Maxim said with a frown. "She had to pretend to be a man, shaving her hair and smoking, until she was discovered. She was from Novgorod. I think she's still at the front, actually. They didn't make her leave. She was pretty good."

"But surely she would have done better working as a nurse if she had to go that far from home," said the General's wife.

I bit my tongue. Elena Stefanovna had always spoken of women as though we were weaker than men. Telling her how strong some of the women at the factory were wouldn't change her way of thinking.

"Some women don't want to be nurses," I said.

"This woman sergeant won't have many volunteers," the actress said, smiling at me with sugar on her lips. "It takes a special kind of woman to—pardon my forwardness here—to take off her skirts and put on men's trousers."

"Many may volunteer," said Captain Lermontov, "but few will stick with it. They don't have the stamina for military training."

Clearly, Lermontov hadn't spent any time in an arms factory. After working in the grenade filling room for the last five months, I'd seen enough female strength and sacrifice to move mountains. One time, a woman threw herself at another, pushing her away just as a crate fell off a shelf. She was crushed, but she'd saved her friend.

"Sir," I said, hoping no one would hear any excitement in my voice. "I think it's a brilliant idea. For those women who have been sneaking into the fight disguised as men, it will save them a haircut."

When they chuckled, I forced myself to join them, though my laugh was as real as the actress's waistline.

The next course was brought in and my mind drifted, dwelling on Sergeant Bochkareva. How had a woman cornered the Minister of War and gotten him to agree to something no one had ever done before? Except the mythical Amazons, no one had raised an all-woman army to fight in battle. Even Saint Olga had used men to do her dirty work.

All was well at the table, and then the General had to ruin

the evening entirely. Once the dessert dishes had been cleared, he asked for a round of vodka to be brought to the table. Then, as we all lifted our glasses, he made a toast.

"To our heroes soon to return to the front." Then he pointed his glass at Maxim and the two shared the darkest of looks. He threw back the glass and drank it all in one gulp, as did everyone around me. I didn't move.

"Maxim?" I asked.

He looked away quickly. Too quickly.

"You didn't tell her yet? You've had two weeks!" The General shook his head. "He's been recalled to the front, my dear. Maxim must report in at the end of the week."

He hadn't told me. It was a punch to the gut. I almost dropped the shot glass.

Everyone was staring at me. If I didn't drink to the toast, I'd be wishing my brother—and all soldiers—misfortune. If I did drink, I'd be agreeing to my brother leaving me again.

I put the glass to my lips. The vodka burned all the way down.

———

On the way out, I asked Elena Stefanovna if I could take a look at her book collection. Thrilled, she brought me from room to room, but to my frustration, she avoided the German room. After she explained to me how Mark Twain was the American version of Leo Tolstoy—which I highly doubted because his books were only half as thick—I mentioned how before the war, I'd been studying foreign languages.

"I'd forgotten about that. You were focused on French and English, am I right?" she asked with a light squeeze on my wrist. "Just like my Ilya."

"French and German, actually. For the chemistry concentration, we had to learn German, not English."

"Oh my. And do you remember any of it? Do you—do you have any friends in Germany?"

"Of course not," I laughed. "Do you mind if I take a look at your collection, though? German books are difficult to find now, you know, and I've heard you have the best collection in the city."

That did the trick. She happily ushered me into a dark-paneled room with two wide bookcases set beneath the tall windows. Altogether, they held perhaps forty books.

She crossed her arms. "It's not such a large collection, really. Mostly philosophy and fables."

"You wouldn't happen to have a copy of *Faust*, would you?"

There was a polite cough in the door behind us, and we both whirled around. Captain Lermontov stood in the doorway, a thin smile on his lips. "A lover of Goethe, are you?"

"She hates old books like that," Maxim said behind him. "Don't you, Katya?"

If I didn't get this done with, I was going to run screaming from the house. "I'm not a little girl anymore," I said to my brother, showing my teeth.

"Well," Elena Stefanovna said. She hurried to the bookcases and pulled out a leather-bound copy. "Here is it, dear."

I took the book and flipped through it as casually as I could. "Who was the better writer, do you think? Goethe or . . ." I racked my brain for another German writer. "Schiller?"

"Schiller," said Maxim. He'd pushed his way past the Captain, who continued to lean against the door frame.

"Do you have any Schiller, Elena Stefanovna?" I asked sweetly.

While she searched the bookcases with Maxim, I pulled a

slip of paper from between the pages and stuck it up my sleeve. Then I caught Lermontov's eye and snapped the book shut. "What about you, Captain?"

"I prefer Goethe, myself. He was quite the educator. May I?" He reached out, and I handed him the book.

I had accomplished what I'd come here to do, and suddenly the stress of the evening caught up with me. Stifling a yawn, I turned to Maxim.

"Maybe you're right. German literature is putting me to sleep."

He chuckled. He must have thought I'd forgiven him for not telling me about his recall. "You haven't even read any of it."

"It is rather late for a factory worker," the Captain said. "She must have to wake early."

He shepherded me out of the room, followed by Maxim and Elena Stefanovna. While we retrieved our coats, I saw the Captain flipping the pages of the book. It was done.

"Maxim Viktorovich, you take care when you get back to the front," Elena Stefanovna said. She wrapped her arms around him and kissed him on the cheeks. "Come back safe."

My hand was hard as concrete in the crook of Maxim's arm as we left the General's house. We were only a step apart, but it felt like an entire field of barbed wire had been strung up between us.

"Why didn't you tell me?" I asked as soon as we rounded the corner.

"I was hoping I wouldn't have to."

"What were you going to do? Wait until you were packed up ready to go? And I would see you in uniform again and cry, 'Oh, Maxim! My heroic brother!'"

He yanked his arm away from mine.

Blood boiled in my veins, and I couldn't cool it down. I didn't want to. Months of taking care of him, of saving up to pay off his mistakes, of haggling for real tea so he'd have something to drink that wouldn't rot his liver—and he still treated me like a child. A child who couldn't handle difficult news.

"I wrote to Papa." His voice was tight, like he was forcing it through a narrowing pipe. "I said you needed me here, and that I wasn't ready to go back. I even brought up how if I left, it would be like Mama abandoning us, all over again. Remember how hard it was? But he didn't do a damn thing to help. And when I went to General Yudenich, he showed me the stack of Ilya's letters. Ilya!" His lips trembled. "He threw my best friend's letters in my face, going on and on about how his son had given *everything* for Russia and I was nothing but a wet chicken. All his talk about my bravery at dinner tonight, that was for you. When it was just him and me, he was a cold bastard."

"You know how they idolized Ilya," I said quietly. He seemed not to hear.

"I didn't tell you because I was hoping for something else. Even a posting here in Petrograd. Anything but to go back there." He shivered.

I should have taken his hand in mine, but both of us were carrying tight fists, our knuckles locked in worry and frustration. We marched home this way, swinging our fists like the soldiers we weren't.

"Olga was married to Prince Igor of Kiev, who collected tribute from his people along the river."

"What's a tribute?"

"Money for keeping them safe. One year, he went to collect a very high tribute from Prince Mal. When Igor went back and asked for more, Mal had him killed."

"How?"

"How did they kill him?"

"Yes. With swords? With arrows? Did they decapitate him?"

"How do you—I'm going to talk with your brother."

4

APRIL 18, 1917

"**PAVLOVA!**" The shrill cry of my name carried over the metallic clanging of grenade trays being set onto the worktables. I stilled, my emptied scoop resting on the finger-wide rim of the grenade's cavity. As cleanly as I could, I set the scoop down and turned to face the forewoman. The other girls on the line continued working, not wanting to miss their quotas.

Natalya Ivanovna filled the doorway with her hands on her hips. Her usual gray kerchief was replaced with a wool one with large pink roses, but her frown was the same weary line as always. Behind her stood three men, one with a pair of wire glasses on his nose, and the others with clipboards. I'd never seen them before.

"Yes, Natasha Ivanovna?" I asked.

She cocked her head at the men behind her. "You're to come with us."

"Is something wrong?" She didn't look upset with me in particular, but something was definitely stirring up her skirt.

"Other than the war?" she snapped. Then, with a resigned sigh, she pinched the bridge of her nose. "We have a new grenade model to discuss." With that, she turned and waited for the men to part, allowing her through. They followed behind her, none of them giving me a second glance.

I wiped my hands on a cloth and followed, cursing the fact that I wouldn't make quota today, which meant my pay would be docked. Natasha Ivanovna took the men into the education room, and I entered to find all the other line leaders already present. The other girls and women stood behind waist-high tables, shoulder to shoulder, not a one of them looking the least bit pleased at being taken from their lines either. Masha stood in the middle of the room with her hand covering the table space beside her. When she saw me, she waved me over, ignoring the mumbling from another woman who'd wanted the space.

"Any ideas?" she asked, keeping her voice low.

"A new model?" I whispered with a shrug.

Natasha Ivanovna and the three men came to stand at the front of the room, facing us. She motioned to one of the younger girls to shut the door, and then the man in the glasses cleared his throat.

"My name is Pyotr Pavlovich Guchkov," he began, with more enthusiasm than I'd expected from a man who looked like he hadn't slept since the war began. "I'm an engineer at the university. I know some of you from the smelting room." He nodded at a group of women along the wall, all metalworkers. "We brought you in here today to discuss the next stage of the M1914 grenade. The plans are finally finished, thanks to these men from the chemistry department."

Pyotr Pavlovich motioned to the back of the room, and I turned to see a boy standing behind a giant projector. "Cut the lights," Pyotr Pavlovich said. Then he and the others parted to clear space on the newly whitewashed wall. The boy started the projector, and a diagram of the M1914 lit up the darkness.

"This is the current model you all know and love."

Masha snickered beside me, and I bumped my shoulder into hers.

Pyotr Pavlovich's dry voice carried across the darkened room. "It works well, but we have been ordered to make a more effective weapon. After months of research, and with some help from the British, we are ready to begin making the newer model. It is called the M1917G. You may wonder what the G stands for." He paused for dramatic effect, and it worked. No one made a peep. "It is what changes everything: gas."

A low murmur snaked through the rows of women.

"Chloropicrin," Natasha Ivanovna explained in a sharp tone, shutting down the whispers and comments. "The grenade will release chloropicrin gas."

"Precisely," said Pyotr Pavlovich. "It does not explode like a TNT grenade, but it can be more effective. As far as it concerns you in the factory, it shall be treated with the same care as the TNT. It will not explode, it will not tint you yellow, but if you are not careful, it will kill you and those around you." This particular news was for me, for my line. "The majority of you will see no change in your work. As you can see, the grenade's body is nearly the same."

One of the other men motioned to Pyotr Pavlovich, and the boy in the back clicked the projector, displaying the chemical components of the gas.

Natasha Ivanovna pulled open the door. "Those of you not in the explosives line may return to your work. We will begin training shortly." Most of the women filed out, including Masha, leaving just a few of us behind.

One of the chemists pointed at the projected information. "As you can see, this will be far less dangerous for you than what you're currently filling the canisters with. With care, you will find it much more pleasant to work with."

I wanted to laugh, but there was no one to share it with now that Masha was gone. Everyone else was hard-faced, studying the information on the wall.

A woman raised her hand. "When will we start?"

"Tomorrow," the chemist said. "The gas will arrive this afternoon. Pyotr Pavlovich will be here after the shift ends to assist any of you if you have questions. And if you wish, he can show you what you must do. If you cannot stay late, I will instruct you tomorrow."

No one asked why we were upgrading from basic explosives to gas-filled weapons. After nearly three years of war, Russia had yet to bring the Germans and Austrians to their knees. Meanwhile our own soldiers had been gassed. The casualties of this technology arrived weekly on the trains from the front, filling hospitals to the brim, reminding us how badly we were outmatched.

I studied the image of the grenade and the technical details, trying to imprint it into my brain. I wasn't going to wait until tomorrow to learn how to make this new horror.

The Kazan Cathedral was not Petrograd's largest or most opulent cathedral, but it did look the most Roman. Or so my babushka told me. The last time I'd come here had been with her. After my mother left, she had taken me to all the cathedrals and larger churches in the city. Anywhere someone noble had been born. She said it was to teach me to honor Russia's past, but I was pretty sure she had a secret list of every Saint Georgi icon in the city because there seemed to be one everywhere we went. She would always go straight to it, sketch the sign of the cross and give it a kiss. Then, she'd covertly pull out a scrap of paper and tick something off with a pencil stub.

The Kazan Cathedral's two colonnades reached out from the green dome as if embracing the park and fountain in front. At this time of night, when the sun was gone but still cast a subtle glow across the sky, the spaces between the columns were rich with shadow and silence. It was behind the seventh column on the northern side that I was to meet Sergei.

A small group of men clustered at the end of the opposite colonnade, but they were preoccupied with a bottle of vodka and paid no attention to me.

I stepped up into the shadows. My heart leapt to my throat, and its rapid beating only increased my awareness. I was not safe here in the near-dark. This was a terrible time to meet anyone, much less a Bolshevik. If only I'd been here on time, before sunset.

Counting the columns, I trod quietly. The light here was soft, brushing the outside edge of the northernmost columns with filtered gold—strangely peaceful despite the deep shadows.

I heard a faint, sour chuckle and froze in place.

"I've had to brush off two advances from would-be lovers." Sergei's voice came from the darkness before he stepped into the fading light.

"I'm sorry I'm late."

He shrugged. "I was still here."

"I—here." I handed him the note I'd found in the copy of *Faust*.

"Thanks." It disappeared somewhere in his jacket. "So why were you late? Extra shift at the capitalist war factory?"

I frowned, choosing to ignore his jab. "It just took me a while to get out of there today."

He raised an eyebrow, a neat trick that I had never been able to manage. "Were you with your really tall friend?"

"Masha. She's not that tall. Just taller than I am."

"I like tall girls."

"Speaking of girls," I said, "the army might be forming an all-women's battalion."

"Women soldiers? Really?"

"Don't sound so surprised. You told me the Bolsheviks believe women should have equal rights. That we're just as smart and capable as men."

"And you are. I'm just surprised the Provisional Government agrees with us. Did you hear about this at the party the other night?"

I nodded as I scanned the area around us again, making sure we weren't going to be accosted by anyone. "I don't know if it will actually happen. It's just an idea that's been brought up. The army is having a problem with morale."

He grinned, looking absolutely cocky. "We've been passing out copies of *Pravda* to the soldiers at the front, because the best thing for Russia—and the revolution—is for the war to end. We need to turn our backs on the Germans and focus on ourselves."

I couldn't agree. Commitment in a time of war had been bred into me alongside my nightly prayers. It was all I could do to tuck away the bit of guilt I felt around my work for the Bolsheviks, but that wasn't abandoning the war or the causes that we were fighting for. I was sharing information with our own people. I wasn't asking our men to leave their comrades in the midst of battle.

"I don't like war either, but we can't wave a white flag and expect Germany to hand us back our borders with a smile and a barrel of beer."

"If only it could be so easy." He seemed to be studying a stray lock of my hair. "You'll see in time. Their plots won't work, and in the end, Russia will be stronger. Now, before I go, I've brought this for you." He reached into the other side of his jacket and pulled out an envelope, which he handed to me.

It was smooth and cool in my hand, the edges sharp. I could easily picture the cash inside. "Thank you."

"If you can get more information about the women's battalion, we would appreciate it."

"I'll try. My brother leaves this week for the front." The words were dry as chalk on my tongue. "Once he's gone, I'll have more freedom. You could meet me at my apartment on Wednesdays, when our housekeeper doesn't come."

His eyes glinted in the lamplight. "To receive information?" he asked.

"Of course." I blushed and was grateful for the dark.

"I wish your brother well, despite how I feel about the war. You know I mean for our soldiers to come home so that no more lives are lost, right?"

"I know. It's what we all want. An end."

"Ah, but you want that end to be glory in battle, flags waving and trumpets blaring, and I want the end of the war no matter the cost."

My mind flashed with the image of our white, red, and blue flag flying over an endless stretch of bodies, and I felt a little sick. "Goodnight, Sergei."

His fingers flexed as if he were about to reach toward me, but he kept his hand at his side. "Till next time."

———

Inserting a poisonous gas into a narrow chamber was not as exciting as I'd expected. The gas smelled like fly paper, and within minutes, my eyes stung. Everyone teared up despite the goggles, and since our hands were occupied, we wiped our damp cheeks on our shoulders.

Natasha Ivanovna, always present when we were doing something new, stood by the closed door, ready to pull it open should any of us make a fatal mistake. She held the corner of her kerchief over her mouth, as though her homespun wool provided some sort of protection.

I focused on the canister of chloropicrin I was holding. A bare skull was painted onto the side, half covered by my thumb. It was cold to the touch, almost painfully cold. Carefully, I lifted the canister and set the lid against the funnel propped into the grenade. It was an oily gas, and poured softly. I blinked back tears and made sure to stop at the right moment.

Fill, stopper, next one. Fill, stopper, next one. On and on until my stomach couldn't stand the fumes one second longer. Keeping my hands as steady as I could manage, I set down my tools and raced out into the hall. Someone had wisely set up a few buckets, one of which I made my own as I vomited, gasping the fresh, clean air from the hall and weeping out the sting of the gas.

A hand squeezed my shoulder. "I'm getting you better masks." It was Natasha Ivanovna. "They say they'll be here next week. Until then, try to get as many filled as you can."

I nodded because I still could not speak. Her footsteps faded down the hall until it was only me and my bucket. My throat ached.

I couldn't do this anymore.

But I had to. I pushed myself up, wiped at my cheeks, and went back inside the room.

There might be a battalion just for women. The news invaded my thoughts. Women were being given a chance to fight. They didn't have to beg for one or disguise themselves like the woman who'd fought in Maxim's unit.

At the end of the day, I changed back into my skirt and blouse. Back into my shoes with laces, back into my hairpins and metal-framed stays, all of which were forbidden in the filling stations. Each layer transformed me back into the young woman I pretended to be on the street. Ekaterina Viktorovna Pavlova, the colonel's daughter. Secret messenger for the Bolsheviks. Sister to an unlucky gambler who was returning to the war.

Masha was in the dressing room, ready to go outside. Her new hat with the silk peonies rested on her head, stuck into her hair with a pin as long as my hand, a gift from Masha's Siberian grandmother. I'd never seen her leave home without it.

She gave me a curious look, with one of her barely-there brows lifted so high it was hidden beneath the brim.

"You look gassy," she said with a smirk.

"Funny." I re-braided my hair and tied it with a strip of linen. Then I pulled on my jacket. It was chilly outside, even though it was late April. "Do you think it will help?"

"The new grenades? Sure. How couldn't they? Finally, our soldiers will have modern weapons. It has to do something."

"But will it be enough?"

Masha tucked a lace shawl around her shoulders and tied it off. Her shoulders were high and tense, the only warning I had before she turned to me. "This is about Maxim, isn't it? You're worried about him going back."

"That's not it. I mean, yes, I'm worried. But it's more than that. How will it all end? Will we win? Or will we run for the Steppes, the enemy at our heels?"

"You're asking the wrong person. I can't think past today. It's too hard otherwise! My father is gone to fight. Half of our neighbors are gone too, or sent home wounded. The city has an odd echo, and now that the Tsar isn't in charge, all I hear are cries for another revolution."

My hand shook when I slid my hat pin in, and I nearly jabbed myself in the scalp. "I hear that too."

When we parted ways that afternoon, I couldn't stop thinking about what Sergei had said about me. Was I really the sort of person who wanted victory over peace? And if so, was that so bad?

"Once Prince Igor was dead, Prince Mal decided to marry his widow and kill his infant son."

"Olga couldn't marry the man who killed her husband! And she couldn't let him kill her baby!"

"This is why people remember this story. Because she refused in a rather spectacular fashion."

"How?"

"I know it's hard for you, but please try to be patient while I tell the story."

5

MAY 1, 1917

OVER the next few days, I helped my brother collect and pack his things, both of us too polite, both of us watching the stiff, quick tick of the clock.

The day before he was supposed to report, I caught him pacing in the foyer. "What are you doing?"

He froze, then reached over and pulled the rusty umbrella from where it leaned against the wall. "I was just looking for the umbrella."

"Do you bring an umbrella to war?" I asked, mirroring his insincere smile. I tried not to think about the recent newspaper articles detailing the army's supply shortages. Units were running low on food, rifles, boots, and even smaller gear, like cooking pans and gas masks.

"It might help," Maxim said, swinging the umbrella back and forth jauntily. "I could pop it open and block the bullets."

This was my old brother, the one who'd brought me little bouquets of snowdrops wrapped in string and told me they'd been picked by a *léshy*. I didn't know where he'd come from, but I didn't want him to leave.

"Very stylish," I said. "Mama would be proud."

Instantly his face darkened. We never talked about our mother. "Well, that would be a surprise, wouldn't it?" He jabbed the umbrella at me like a saber, stopping just before it hit my chest. "Think she'd be proud of a son who dies on the battlefield?"

"You won't die," I said, hating the quaver in my voice. "We're making a new grenade . . ."

He lowered the umbrella. "How's that going to help me, Katya? Honestly. The only thing that would help is if Russia quit the war."

"They're gas grenades. They'll be more effective."

"My dear sister," he said, "it'll take more than a few cases of poison gas to push the Germans back to Berlin. It'll take every last Russian standing. And since that won't happen . . ."

He shoved the umbrella back against the wall and was out the door before I could react.

Without the stand to hold it upright, the umbrella slid to the ground and landed with a clatter.

—

MAY 2, 1917

The next morning, I came downstairs to find Maxim in full uniform.

His wide leather holster was weighted down with his pistol, his winter overcoat draped his shoulder, and his buckles shone with fresh polish. He had the rest of his kit wrapped in leather straps and a canvas bag. For a moment, it looked as if he might say something, but instead he gestured at the bench by the front door. We sat down for a moment to fool any bad luck that might come our way. I didn't believe in such silly things, but at the moment, Maxim needed whatever he could get, real or not.

Paulina came from the kitchen with a parcel wrapped in a tea towel and centuries of matronly knowledge. "You'll want something to eat on the train," she said. It was the same thing she'd said when Maxim had left the first time.

"Thanks," Maxim said as he took it and tucked it under an arm. He kissed her cheeks before she retreated from the foyer.

I pointed at Maxim's canvas bag. "Want help with that?"

He lifted his chin. "Go ahead and try."

I rolled my eyes as I got up to grab it. It wasn't light, but I managed to sling it over my shoulder. "This is easier," I grunted, "than moving a case of grenades."

He seemed more like the old Maxim than usual. His steps were lighter, his eyes brighter. It was odd, considering this was the day he was leaving to go back to the front.

"Katyusha." He hadn't called me that in years. "You've been amazing, bringing me back from the dead and helping me . . . And I've been the worst sort of brother."

"Just the normal sort of brother, I think, under the circumstances."

"Right. Let's excuse all sorts of behavior for the sake of the war." We stood there a moment, neither of us knowing what else to say, and then he shook his head, as if clearing away unwanted thoughts. "Let's go."

Outside the apartment, we climbed into the cab he'd arranged for. The sky was covered in thick, ruddy clouds, and the sun cast an oddly unreal light over the street and the accompanying canal. Everything looked falsely lit, as though the poplars, the rows of townhouses, and even the golden pedestrian bridge were all part of a giant's toy train set. All tin and lead paint.

Once Maxim's bag was stowed in the back of the cab, the driver cracked the whip and the horse took us away. I sat frozen, but Maxim twisted in his chair to gaze over his shoulder.

"A last look," he said.

"Don't say that."

The city passed by quickly. By the time we reached the station, the clouds had parted and the sun was spreading out over Petrograd. Everything before me—the hundreds of uniformed soldiers, the wagons loaded with provisions, the colorful civilians running through it all—became a solid, clear crystal. This was truly happening.

I waited on the train station platform while Maxim brought his bag onto the officers' car. When he came out, he moved like he still had the full weight of the kit on his shoulders.

"I suppose this is goodbye." His eyes were on the train.

"They really are forming a women's battalion," I blurted. I didn't know where the thought came from, but it brought his gaze back to the here and now.

He frowned. "You're not thinking of joining that charade, are you?"

Another officer chose that moment to slap Maxim on the shoulder. He was wearing the same regimental insignias, but he had on the uniform of the cavalry.

"Lieutenant Pavlov! I didn't know you'd be coming back." His eyes skirted to me, and he gave us a knowing wink. "Ah, I'll let you say your farewells to your girl, then. Plenty of time to chat on the train."

I expected Maxim to correct him, to tell him I was his little sister, but he just gave the man a nod and turned back to me.

"You don't mean to join, right?" he pressed.

"I don't know. It sounds interesting. I could put all the time I spent watching Papa's battalion to some use."

He shook his head vehemently. "Stay here, out of the way. You can have your grenades, but don't come any closer to the fighting than that. We'll need you here when we get back."

"I'll be here," I said. The platform was emptying up. Time was running out.

His shoulders stiffened, and he looked down the line of train cars. "Take care of yourself, Katya. When you get back, look in my room. I left you something that might help with your new grenades."

I gripped him by the sleeve, suddenly struck with foreboding. "What is it?"

He shrugged. "You'll have to look when you get home." He looked down the line of train cars again. "Take care of yourself, Katya."

I gave him a kiss on each cheek, knowing a hug would get me stuck on his pins, straps, and weaponry. "Take care of yourself."

He gave me a cocky salute and then ducked into the train car, reappearing a moment later at the window where he flattened his palm to the pane. I pressed mine to the cold, dirty glass, aligning my hand with his.

And then the train began to move, and I was left behind.

————

When I got home from the factory that night, I went straight past the covered plate Paulina had left for me on the dining table and into Maxim's room to find whatever it was he'd left behind for me.

I found his rubbery green gas mask staring at me from the middle of his bed.

He'd left it behind for me to use. Gently, I lifted it off its crocheted perch, feeling the weight of it. It smelled strongly of oil and soap, and the lenses were polished and clear. He'd cleaned it for me.

I fitted it over my head. It slipped easily over my braid and pinched my ears, but it fit well enough. The lenses were spaced a bit too wide, as if I was standing at the corner of a building trying to see both sides at once. I sucked in a breath and choked on dust, then sobbed a laugh because there was always something he forgot to do.

With a clean filter, this would protect my lungs while I filled the grenades with gas. I wouldn't spend the day coughing or fighting nausea. I could work faster and make my quota every time. It was the perfect gift.

Except for one thing. I knew from the newspaper reports that the army's supply of gas masks was running low. And Maxim might be an officer, but he was expected to fight alongside his men.

He needed his mask at the front.

"Prince Mal sent his men to Kiev to ask Olga to marry him."

"He didn't go himself?"

"No, and when Olga met his men, she asked if her people could bring them into the city by carrying them in their longboat."

"That's silly."

"Yes, but they were told it was a great honor in Kiev. And they believed her."

6

MAY 15, 1917

THE next few weeks passed without so much as a whisper from Maxim.

A little weed of worry kept growing in the back of my mind, climbing into my nightmares and choking my throat at tea. I knew it was too soon for letters from the front, but I had hoped he would send me something from one of the stops along the way.

And now that Maxim was gone, the letters from our father wouldn't come as often. Not that Papa was a particularly interesting correspondent; his letters were full of complaints about his troops, praises for his attaché, a Lieutenant Sarkovsky whom I'd never met, and the weather. He never asked a single question.

I kept working my shifts at the factory, and pouring the gas had gotten easier with my brother's mask. During breaks, when the girls were talking about their lovers who'd gone to fight, I leaned against the courtyard wall and smoked a borrowed cigarette so that my mouth and hands had something to do. Masha usually left me alone so she could chat with the other paper girls, but today she rested a shoulder on the wall, facing me, and nudged my toe with hers.

"That's two men gone to the front for you."

I didn't say anything.

"It's just that it must be hard. I only have my father over there, and it's enough to ruin my sleep."

I dropped the cigarette and squashed it on the ground. "They're not over there 'for me.' They left because there's a war. I didn't ask them for anything."

"Yes, but they *think* they're doing it for you. They think they're fighting to save you. It's a male instinct that, well, I sometimes understand."

"I don't need saving, Masha. And neither do you."

She kicked at my squashed cigarette until it was nothing but little brown fibers scratched into the dirt. "We all need saving."

At that moment, the metal gate facing the street banged open and a girl in trousers and a school cap sauntered in.

"Who's she?" Masha asked, but no one answered.

The girl moved confidently across the courtyard to where we all stood against the brick wall. She held a stack of papers tucked into her armpit and handed one off to the first person she came to. Before long, she stood before me with a sly smile.

"If you want the war to end, read this and consider."

I took the proffered flyer while she moved on to Masha, then the rest of the women.

"Can everyone read?" the girl asked, spinning around to get a good look at all present. A few women shook their heads, and she marched over to talk to them.

I bent my head over the flyer.

Women of Russia, prove yourselves stronger than the
deserters. You, the spirit and strength of Russia, are needed
at the Front! To fight!
Arise, brave women! . . .
The country has forgotten the honor of soldiers . . .
They are cowards, they are afraid
To defend us with their bayonets.
They have already made peace with the enemy . . .
Arise then for your freedom,
While it is not too late to fight.
You can bring happiness to the people,
Let the men do the washing!

Rally for the Women's Battalion of Death at the
Mariinsky Theater

May 21; 1800 hours.

Masha's fingers were gripping the paper, now crumpled.
"You're going to join, aren't you?" I asked her.

On the other side of me, one of the girls laughed. "I don't
think this is real. Just something put out by the Bolsheviks to
stir up trouble."

"That's not Bolshevik paper," I said, hoping no one would
ask how I knew that. "It's the same kind of paper the army uses
for its official correspondence, I mean."

"It's real." Masha's voice was deep, like the words came
from the darkest part of her. The truest part of her. "And yes.
I will go." She took my hand and covered it with hers. "You
should too."

I gaped at her. For weeks I'd been turning this over in my

62

mind, yet it had only taken Masha seconds to make her choice. It seemed unfair that she should always be so sure of herself. "What makes you say that?"

"Remember when you were taking lessons from Ilya? How you left my birthday party early because that was the one day he could show you how to fight with a saber without you two getting caught by the armory sergeant?"

"I thought you didn't like it when I did that!" She hadn't complained, but she'd never asked to join us—which, for Masha, was usually a clear sign of disapproval.

"Well, I was a little jealous you had so much time alone with Ilya," she said slyly. "But I knew you weren't running off to kiss him."

The thought of Ilya turned my stomach.

Slowly, I slipped my hand out from beneath hers. "I can't go to the rally." My voice came out sharp. My eyes stung and I blinked hard. The flyer had spoken to me, and I *wanted* to go. I wanted to carry a rifle and wear the uniform, and if any woman in Petrograd was ready for it, it was me.

"Why not?"

"All three of us can't be at the front—there'd be no one left at home." If Babushka were still alive, or if my mother had stayed with us, perhaps it would be different. But I'd promised Maxim I would be here when he got back.

"I thought you wanted to help with the war."

"We *are* helping with the war." I forced a smile and made it wicked, hoping to cover the sinking feeling in my chest. "We make the best grenades this side of Paris."

MAY 16, 1917

A ration of bread, cheese, an onion, and three books from Elena Stefanovna's Russian room weighted down my arms as I kicked in the front door to my apartment building. It groaned open, and while I wondered when it had last been oiled, the old guard ran over to help. I shook my head.

"I'm fine."

He was blocking my way to the stairwell. "Ekaterina Pavlova? There's a telegram for you."

The books doubled in weight and the straps of the linen bag dug into my palm like a knife. Telegrams only brought bad news.

He pulled an envelope out of his pocket. "It's from Colonel Pavlov." He held it out for a moment and, when I didn't move, set it on top of the stack of books.

"Thank you." The words were habit, and so were my steps as I made my way around him. The light through the stairwell's yellow glass window, the ivory and black checkered steps, the key in the lock and the bread, cheese, and onion on the floor. The books on the shoe rack, the gray envelope shaking, shaking, ripping open.

I looked at the telegram inside.

```
Maxim did not arrive. Deserter.

          —Col V. Pavlov
```

No one was dead.

I sank onto the floor and curled over the telegram, all the gut-twisting worry draining from me like dishwater, only to be replaced by a dull sick feeling. If I'd heard it from a soldier, or if I'd read it in the paper, I would not have believed it. But Papa never lied, never embellished, and had never sent a telegram in the three years he'd been gone. If Papa said it, it must be so.

I'd been hoarding tears of worry for weeks, fearful that the last I'd ever see of Maxim would be through that grimy train window. But I hadn't expected *this*.

No matter how many times I looked, the type was always the same. Papa's voice grew louder in my ear until he was shouting, his voice carrying across Belarus, over the east of Russia to Petrograd.

My son has deserted! I heard him cry. And then the telegram was spotted and damp, the ink spreading, its barbs branching along the folds. *Now there is no one to stand with me at the front.*

The door had been left open, and a neighbor's steps echoed in the stairwell. With a sharp kick, I shut the door and was alone with a ration of bread, a bit of cheese, an onion, and three leather-covered novels.

Maxim's face in the train window wavered in my mind, his jawline dissolving in the shadowy interior. His palm against the pane. My own hand absorbing the cold of the glass, but somehow also feeling his hand against mine.

It would be the last time together, because Maxim would never come home now. He was not dead, but the scant five words from my father declared Maxim dead *to him*.

"Olga had a deep hole dug inside Kiev's walls, and when her people brought Prince Mal's men—in their boat—she had them dropped into the hole."

"No!"

"Oh yes. Olga leaned down over them and said, 'Have we honored you justly?' Then she had them buried alive."

7

MAY 17, 1917

MASHA didn't show up at the factory the next day. As soon as I clocked out and washed my hands, I made my way across Petrograd to her apartment building, a twenty-minute walk from my own. With each bump of the rails, I wondered what had kept her. She hadn't seemed ill the day before, and she never missed a day otherwise.

The sun perforated a thick clump of dark clouds, scattering weak light across the city. It was chillier than it had been a few hours ago, but I had my shawl and enough anger burning inside to keep me warm whenever I thought of Maxim's desertion and how the war had torn apart my family.

Masha lived on a busier street than the one I grew up on. The buildings were taller, tighter, and cobwebbed with electrical wires crisscrossing the street. Her parents chose this part of town because, according to her father, it had a dynamic culture, and that was where the best ideas were sprung.

I ran the two flights up to her apartment. When I knocked, the front door creaked open of its own accord. There was no one in the hallway, so I let myself in. It was too quiet.

In the parlor, Masha sat on the sofa beside her mother, both of them drained of life. They were like paper dolls, in fine clothes but pale and stiff.

Relief that Masha wasn't ill gave way to dread when I noticed the telegram in Masha's mother's lap. "What happened?" I took the seat opposite from them.

"It's Papa," Masha croaked. "He's in a hospital somewhere near Riga. They don't—" She hiccupped and clapped a hand over her mouth.

My stomach plummeted. "I am so sorry, Masha." I wrapped an arm around her shoulders and squeezed.

Her mother, Sabina Andreyevna, looked as if she would never move again. She didn't even blink. Her face was edged in sadness the way rose petals fade and darken as they die. "He could already be dead, and we wouldn't know," she said faintly.

"They'll wire you as soon as they know something more," I said, although I didn't believe that. The army was notorious for taking weeks, or even months, to let families know what had happened. In some cases, they claimed a soldier had disappeared in battle, never to be seen again.

And sometimes they sent a telegram with a five-word message.

Sabina Andreyevna sat up straight. "I am going to him."

"Mama, no. It's too far."

"Masha is right," I added. "And they won't let you in unless you're a nurse."

Sabina Andreyevna bent over, clutching at her stomach. "I can't sit here and do nothing," she cried. "I can't."

"Write to him. It would get there faster than you could, and someone will read it to him if he can't do it himself," I said. "My brother—" My voice hitched, but I pressed on. "My brother said that they never failed to bring him my letters when he was in the hospital. They were the only things he had to look forward to." I looked away, unable to face Masha. I'd come to tell her about Maxim, but now was not the time.

"We'll write to him tonight and send it first thing tomorrow, Mama. We don't know if I'll be . . ." Masha trailed off, sounding suddenly unsure.

"I can't believe you're still going to join that woman! Knowing what has happened to your father!"

"Are you still signing up?" I squeaked. "For the women's battalion?"

"Mama," she said, ignoring my question, "the danger hasn't grown any greater since we received the telegram. And Papa will get better." She turned to me. "Won't he, Katya?"

I felt sick, but I nodded.

"But what about you?" Sabina Andreyevna's voice wavered, like she was afraid to choose a direction for her fear. "How can I allow my daughter to fight? What if I lose you both?"

"I'm more afraid to stay here and, as you said, Mama, *do nothing*," Masha snapped.

Sabina Andreyevna's eyes flashed up to me. "Are you going too, Katya?"

Masha grabbed my wrist. "Say you'll come with me. Just to the assembly."

I rested my elbows on my knees and stared at the coffee table as if I could see beyond it, through the stones of Petrograd and into the wooden piles the city was built upon. We were a strange line of women, crying over the wounded in one breath and talking of joining the fight in the other.

My father had no one to stand with him at the front.

Perhaps I could prove to him that I didn't have to be a man to be a good soldier.

I nodded. "I'll go the assembly."

"Katya, dear, you don't have to just because Masha wants to!"

"It's not that, Sabina Andreyevna. I want to do more for the war effort; I want to have a purpose. And there's no reason for me to stay in Petrograd any longer."

Sabina Andreyevna took my other hand and wrapped it in hers. "Because your brother went back to the front and you're all alone."

Her hands were soft and smelled of rose water.

"My brother deserted."

The silence was light and fragile, and Masha smashed it to shards. "Damned Germans and their poisonous propaganda!"

"What do you mean?" I asked.

"I read it in the newspaper. The German planes drop leaflets encouraging our soldiers to retreat, to run away. They say they'll be merciful with those that desert, but not with those that fight. The article said it's working, too."

"Another reason General Kerensky agreed to this Women's Battalion scheme, I expect," Sabina Andreyevna said. "If our women go to war, our men will have to stay or be shamed forever."

"I wouldn't go to shame our Russian men," I said. "I would go because I don't want to wait for them all to come home in boxes."

Sabina Andreyevna's face turned to a mask of forced fortitude. "You are the bravest girls I know. It tears my heart into pieces to think of you in the middle of the fight, but I . . . Let me get the vodka."

As soon as she left the room, Masha scooted closer to me. "You don't have to join. Truly."

"I wouldn't join because of you." I jabbed her lightly in the ribs. "And I haven't decided yet. Let's see what happens at the assembly."

"I couldn't bear it if something happened to you, Katya. Why don't you stay and take care of my mother?"

"If you want your mother taken care of, stay for her yourself."

Sabina Andreyevna returned with the vodka and three crystal glasses. She poured us each a tiny bit, but her hands shook and it sloshed onto the rug.

"It's a good thing it's clear." She handed me my glass. It was barely bigger than a thimble, and I held it delicately between my thumb and forefinger.

"To the women of Russia," Masha said.

"To the women," I said.

"To Russia," Sabina Andreyevna said.

We drank, and the vodka burned away the sour taste I'd had on my tongue since I read the word *deserter*.

"Olga sent a message to Prince Mal asking for an escort to his city for their marriage."

"Did he know about the men in the boat?"

"I don't know. But he sent his men to Olga, and she asked them to come to her after they had bathed."

"They must have smelled bad."

"Perhaps. Hygiene wasn't as important then."

"What did they bathe with?"

"These men never took that bath, unfortunately."

"Why? Did she have them killed too?"

"She locked them in the bathhouse and had it set on fire."

"Buried alive and now burned alive! What did she do next?"

"You're more bloodthirsty than I'd thought. Maybe we should talk about Saint Kirill and the alphabet instead."

"Papa!"

8

MAY 21, 1917

THE Mariinsky Theater was, to some people in Petrograd, the jewel of society. Although it was famous for its gilded balconies, it was the people who came that made it unforgettable. The Tsar's family used to sit in the heavily curtained central balcony and peer down at the ballet, although I'd not seen them the one time I'd gone as a child. My mother brought me—*just* me—to see the new ballet, *Swan Lake*. I was unaware that she knew the handsome man seated beside her, until a week later when she left the city with him, never to return.

The Mariinsky had been tainted by the memory of her ever since, and I'd managed to avoid it until today.

Hundreds of women stood where the seats usually were, with barely a space to breathe between them, and with this many people in one place, I almost didn't want to go in. The air was thick with perfume, sweat, and candle wax. A golden brocade curtain hung over most of the stage, leaving a good two meters of space for the lonely podium in the center.

Masha shoved into me as we were finding a spot, and I pressed into her shoulder for a heartbeat before saying,

"Everyone here is either a war widow or too rough to be a nurse."

"Not true," she said, and patted her hair for good measure. "*We're* here, as well as a quarter of the factory women from Petrograd. And I think a peasant woman would make a better nurse than a noblewoman would, anyway. Can you imagine Grand Duchess Anastasia Nikolayevna holding a bed pan?" Her humor had returned, thanks to the telegram she and her mother had received this morning, notifying them of her father's imminent arrival in Petrograd.

There was a wave of movement to our left, where women were passing a stack of paper into the crowd. The gray sheets fanned out quickly, and I wasn't able to snatch one before they were all gone.

"What does it say?" Masha asked, but the woman beside me had trembling hands, causing the words to shake, so I only caught a few words.

When a soldier came on stage, everyone fell silent. It was a grenadier lieutenant, if his epaulets were truly green and not a trick of stage lighting, and he dragged his right leg a little. With each hiss of his boot on the stage, my heart pounded louder. This was real. This was a rally for women to *join the army*.

He cleared his throat and came to a position behind the podium.

"Ladies and gentlemen," he began.

Someone called out, "What gentlemen?" and several women laughed. There were admittedly few men present on the house floor.

"Yes, well," he continued, "the Provisional Government welcomes you tonight."

"Is he a soldier or a circus ring leader?" someone muttered, which sent another row of women tittering. I frowned, not because I had made up my mind to join the army but because whatever would be said tonight would be monumental and these women were making light of it. Or perhaps they were nervous.

"Before we begin, I must introduce you to the person behind this evening's event." The Lieutenant raised his right arm, and a woman in uniform marched onstage. "Sergeant Maria Bochkareva."

Sergeant Bochkareva filled her starched uniform with energy and confidence. Her hair was cut close to the scalp like a common soldier's, but her mouth was soft, small, and serious. She wore several medals pinned across her chest, including an orange-and-black Cross of Saint Georgi for valor in battle. She snapped to attention at the podium, clicking her heels with a crack that carried across the theater.

"Women of Russia!" she shouted. "It is time for us to prove ourselves. To prove our strength and courage!"

"She's right to the point, isn't she?" Masha whispered. I nodded but didn't take my eyes off the stage.

"You are the spirit and strength of Russia, and you are needed at the front," the sergeant called. "Not as nurses, but to fight! Not as a lone woman in a band of brothers, but with your sisters-in-arms! General Kerensky has given me the authority to lead a battalion that will not turn and flee when facing the enemy. My battalion will show our Russian men what it truly means to defend one's country with honor."

She waited a moment, staring out into the crowd with eyes as sharp and clear as a hawk's. Even with her harsh peasant accent, she had hold of the entire house. "I joined the war as soon as I was able, but because I was a woman, I needed a telegram from the Tsar himself—which I obtained. I have been wounded twice in battle, but still I am not afraid. I will go back to the front! I will go to keep our lands free of the Germans. And this time, some of you will come with me."

I could barely take in a breath. Never, in all the time I'd spent with my father's soldiers, had I seen anyone like her. Other soldiers, my brother included, were trying to avoid returning to the front. But she was eager.

I wondered what sort of soldier I would be if I enlisted. Would I be like her, or would I cower?

Her eyes, scanning the crowd, stopped at mine. The hairs on the back of my neck rose at once, and I was caught in her gaze until she blinked and continued looking out at the other women present. She smiled, and her cheeks turned rosy. "I do believe some of you came only to see the novelty of a woman in uniform. Or maybe to see if the rumors were true. But there are women here with the blood and strength of Russia in their veins and *these* are the women I am speaking to tonight."

Suddenly, I needed to know which one she thought I was. I stole a glance at Masha, but she only had eyes for the sergeant. Her mouth hung open slightly.

The speech continued, gaining volume and energy. A parade of women came on stage, some belonging to the Women's Council, others in infantry uniforms who'd had experience fighting alongside men, and one who didn't speak Russian at all but was there representing women's rights—an Englishwoman named Pankhurst. All of them, some with the help of a translator, made the same point: for Russia to be victorious, the women would need to pick up the rifles our men had tossed to the ground in fear.

While the theater echoed in calls to arms and someone shouted questions about pay and training, Masha poked me in the ribs.

"Well?" she whispered. "Are you going to sign up?"

I did not want to wait any longer, alone in the apartment, for this endless war to end. I wanted to do something.

"Yes." With that one word, my veins flashed with fire and I was alive. I was ready.

MAY 25, 1917

I was coming home from my last day at the factory when someone called my name just as I put my hand on the door.

"I didn't know when you'd show up tonight." It was Sergei's voice. I whirled around. He was leaning against a lamppost, bathed in electric light. "I might have a bit of work for you tomorrow night."

"I can't."

He pulled himself away from the lamppost. There was an alarming furrow between his brows. "You can't, or you won't?"

"I won't be able to, because I'll be in training."

"Training." It was a question. "For the new grenades?"

"Army training." The words themselves felt almost as unreal as the idea, rolling off my tongue like lines in a play.

"You're joining the women's death battalion," he said. "The never-wave-the-white-flag suicide battalion. Of women."

"That one." I brushed my hair out of my eyes. "I knew you wouldn't like it."

"It's stupid. The whole thing is stupid. It's a ploy. A stunt." His jaw tensed, and I knew he was trying to hold back his temper.

"It's not a stunt. The war is real, the enemy is real, the

threat is real! And our soldiers are deserting by the thousands. Someone has to pick up their discarded weapons!"

"And it'll only succeed in getting more people killed! The entire point of the death battalions and the shock battalions is to re-energize the war. To keep it going. Our soldiers are refusing to fight because they're finally realizing they're playthings, being sacrificed in the capitalists' game of conquest and power. And you want to be a part of that?"

I would not argue with him, not here and not now. "If that's how you see it."

He cursed under his breath. "How can you not see it like that? You know what needs to happen for the revolution to continue. Ousting the Tsar was just the beginning. The Provisional Government has hardly changed anything. It's shamelessly capitalist, leeching our men—and now women—and pouring their blood on the battlefields in tribute to riches and power."

"So, to be clear," I said, my voice cold, "your problem is not that they're forming a women's death battalion, but that they're forming *any* special battalions? That they're trying to keep Russia in the war? It's not because I'm a *woman*?" I knew I was baiting him, but I couldn't help myself.

"God, Katya! Yes, it's because you're a woman that I'm upset, but not because I don't think you'd make a damned good fighter. I don't doubt some women can be as strong as men. But I don't want you to go." He paused and rubbed at his forehead. "I don't want you to die over something as stupid as this war."

I looked up and smiled in spite of myself. "I could as easily die filling a grenade."

"It's not the same."

"Isn't it? Making grenades is supporting the war. I don't know if it's any more or less helpful than being an actual soldier, but I'm not going to dwell on that right now. My brother deserted, Sergei. He got on that train and then got right off again when no one was looking. Soon enough, everyone will know that Colonel Pavlov's son is a deserter. If he's ever found, his life is over. There are no allowances for deserting lieutenants, you know, even with the Provisional Government's newer, softer army."

We stood there for several heartbeats, glaring at each other.

"Then you're joining the army to make up for what your brother has done?" He asked, without any blame or anger now. As though he'd given up. The sound of his voice twisted something in my stomach. I couldn't look at him.

"No. Maybe. But it's not the only reason."

"What's the other one?"

For a second, I hesitated. Every other reason I'd come up with before—making my father proud or convincing the male soldiers they should do their duty to Russia—didn't sound convincing enough for Sergei. He wouldn't understand being left behind by everyone I'd loved. And then, thinking of Ilya, I knew what to say. "Because I'll be good at it."

His laugh was sour. "Of course." He was suddenly only a hand's breadth away. It was the closest we'd ever been, and with his eyes on my mouth, I was sure he'd try to kiss me. But he leaned over to my ear and whispered, "Keep an eye out for my mark, in case my comrades need you for something."

He stepped back into the streetlight's hazy beam, gave me a mocking salute, and turned around. I watched him saunter down the street until a drink cart passed between us and I lost sight of him.

PART TWO
SOLDIER

"There is scarcely a town or school in Russia from which boys have not run away to the war. Hundreds of girls have gone off in boys' clothes and passed themselves off as boys and enlisted as volunteers, and several have got through, since the medical examination is only a negligible formality required in one place, forgotten in another."

—Stephen Graham, *Russia and the World*, 1915

"After the fire, Olga went to Prince Mal's city herself."

"Did he ask about his men?"

"She told him they were following behind her."

"She was crafty."

"Yes, but lying is a sin. Don't forget."

"If she was so sinful, how'd she get to be a saint?"

"That's a different story. This is before, remember? Anyway, she asked Mal's men if she could have a funeral feast to honor her husband Igor."

"Uh-oh."

"You're catching on quicker than Prince Mal did."

9

MAY 28, 1917

IT was my turn. I walked up to the man sitting behind the typewriter, my limbs jolty from either nerves or excitement. Or both. The soldier's mustache was thinner than a mouse's tail and he was young. He asked my name.

"Ekaterina Viktorovna Pavlova."

He started to type it in and then froze. "Colonel Viktor Pavlov's daughter?"

"We're a family of soldiers." I pinched at the hem of my blouse, hoping he wouldn't have heard yet of my brother. Bureaucracy I could live with, but not pity.

"Does he—uh—do you have permission from *him* to join the army?"

My stomach was cramping, and I crossed my arms over it. "Do I need permission?"

He shuffled the stack of papers, but he wasn't looking at them. "If you're under twenty, you do."

I gritted my teeth. Boys as young as sixteen could join the army without their parents' permission. As in everything else, women were reined in and controlled.

"My father left when the war began. I am independent of him. Of any family," I said, thinking for a second of Maxim, of the bond that had drawn us together for so long. "I know my father will be pleased if I fight." I hoped he would be proud.

"Private Moldov, is there a problem with this recruit?" Sergeant Bochkareva asked, stepping up to the table. Her voice was richer than I'd remembered from the theater, but it still barked loudly across the courtyard.

"She is underage, Sergeant, and doesn't have written permission from her parents."

Sergeant Bochkareva's irritation shone in her eyes.

"My father is already at the front," I said, "and my mother is gone. I have no one to get permission from."

"Her father is—" began the soldier.

"I heard who her father is!" Bochkareva snapped. "I'll ask again: is there a problem with this recruit?"

He gulped and looked at his fingers resting on the typewriter. "Do you have any physical ailments which may prevent you from joining the army?" he asked.

"I do not."

The stamp was loud enough to make me flinch as he slammed it on my recruitment form.

After a humiliating hour of being prodded by doctors in places I'd never been prodded before, I waited against the wall with all the other recruits. Some turned away before they reached the typewriters, their eyes full of doubt and fear. Others swallowed that fear and took another step forward. And still others were sent away by the doctors, either too ill or too pregnant to fight. Sergeant Bochkareva made her rounds between our group and those still in the line, occasionally shouting out to the crowd, claiming we had been called to save Russia.

We were the last hope. We would knock the Germans on their backs.

The energy grew, and I couldn't help but allow it to build up in my own body. We were all excited. We were going to be soldiers, and we'd be right beside the men at the front.

Masha bumped into my shoulder. "Do you think we'll all make it?"

"Through training?" I asked.

She picked at her nails, probably noticing they were too long for what we were about to do. "No. Do you think she's right? That we'll win? That we'll survive?"

"Of course." I squeezed her hand. "I'll watch your back, and you'll watch mine. We'll be fine."

Once the last woman was finished, Sergeant Bochkareva had us line up in four long rows that spanned the width of the courtyard. It took at least five minutes to get everyone quiet and in a somewhat straight line. Some of the women were quick to tell others where to stand, and there was a bit of a scuffle between two women in factory skirts. Sergeant Bochkareva was there in less time than it takes to freeze spit in winter, pulling them apart. She screamed at them and shoved them back into line.

"Women!" she shouted. "I applaud you on your bravery, but don't be stupid! You are here to become soldiers. I will train you. And you will listen to every single word I say." She paused, and the echo of her voice disappeared in the courtyard. "From this moment forward, you will do everything I say. You will run when I say to run. You will crawl when I say to crawl. And you will shoot when I say to shoot."

The lines wavered as hundreds of women shifted on their feet. We filled the courtyard to the metal gate, and the low hum of hundreds of confused voices drowned out the last few words Bochkareva had said.

"Quiet!" Bochkareva shouted. "Take your things to the barracks and report to the barber in twenty minutes. The privates will guide you in the right direction."

The lines started to break apart, and some women literally ran to the barracks, no doubt to find the best beds.

A wiry woman with a Tatar accent asked, "Why do we need a barber?"

I hadn't considered it till this moment, but now it made perfect sense. Bochkareva's own hair was shorn clear to her scalp. I leaned toward the woman and answered, "We have to cut off our hair."

"But why? We can put it up." She patted her tightly coiled knot at the nape of her neck as if to prove her point.

"It'll still get in the way," Masha said, pulling me toward the barracks.

"Imagine getting shot because your hair got caught in the barbed wire," I called over my shoulder.

The barracks were already teeming with women, and we made our way to the back, beside one of the windows. Metal benches with wooden boards laid across them were lined up along the walls, and for a moment we stood there, staring at them. There were no mattresses.

"What are we sleeping on, then? Those?" asked a woman, gesturing with her chin at the benches. Before we could think too deeply on it, we each grabbed one for ourselves.

I slid my two bags of belongings beneath my wooden board. There weren't any lockers, like in my brother's barracks. Of course, his was for officer cadets. They had mattresses and pillows.

"Come," a woman said, "We only have two more minutes." She was the Tatar woman who had asked me about cutting our hair.

The three of us made our way through the clusters of other women, young and middle-aged, who didn't seem to care about the time, and eventually found the hall with the barbers. There were five of them, with women lining up behind each chair, waiting.

The atmosphere had taken on that of a church. Many of us couldn't help but pat our hair or finger the ends of our braids. I'd never thought much about my hair, but soon it would be trimmed off like a tree branch. My gut churned with a strange regret, but also with anticipation. Shaving our hair would be the first step to becoming genuine soldiers.

Sergeant Bochkareva was at the chairs, arms stiff at her side. When it was time, she raised an arm above us to quiet the few whispers.

"You wonder why you must have your head shaved," she said. "Women keep their hair long. It is a feminine right. But from this day forward, you are no longer a woman. You're a soldier. And soldiers do not have braids or hairpins. They shear their hair so they can fight without distraction. They keep it short to look sharp in their uniforms. And so you too, my brave recruits, will join the ranks of thousands who have done this before." She pointed at the handful of recruits at the front of the lines. "Come."

The chosen women walked reverently to the seats. The barbers draped them with cloths, then with one hand on the length of hair and one holding a pair of scissors, cut through years of femininity. Once the hair was short enough, they picked up clippers and sheared off the rest.

"Like sheep," Masha said.

I nodded.

"It will grow back," the Tatar woman said. "After the war."

"I hear it grows a bit even after you're dead," I said, and immediately regretted the words as a few girls around me gasped. "Sorry."

"That's not true, and you know it," Masha said, grinning.

When it was my turn, I steeled myself. I didn't even like my hair that much. It was limp and fine, and anyway, as the other woman said, it would grow back. It was worth it not to end up stuck in barbed wire. But there was a feeling of finality about it, because once our heads were shaved, everyone would know we'd joined the women's battalion.

The barber snipped my braid and my head was suddenly lighter. Then the shears started to chop at the rest, and within a few seconds, my scalp was cold and naked. I stepped away, rubbing at my head like every other woman before me. It tickled my palm.

Masha's eyes seemed to have doubled in size now that her hair was gone. We looked more like tuberculosis patients than soldiers.

"What?" she asked with a laugh. "Do I look as funny as you?"

"If they put you on the posters, no one would fight us. You'd scare the enemy to death."

She chuckled, then showed me her braid, coiled up on her palm. "I saved it for mama."

After our shearing, we ate an early dinner of fish soup and bread at tables set up in an empty hall. Our voices carried, but most of us spoke in hushed tones, still breathing an air of reverence. Or perhaps fear. This was our first meal together. From now on, everything would be different.

When the food was gone, we were taken to a warehouse to receive our uniforms, boots, and a single sheet for our bedding. We carried it all back to the barracks and dropped it on our benches.

We were issued two wool shirts, two pairs of wool trousers, two pairs of stockings, and an overcoat for winter. We were also given special insignia for joining a battalion that fought to the death: skull-and-crossbones emblems and chevrons of black and red. All of it looked too big for me, but it would fit Masha well enough.

While we were going through the items, the woman who had followed us came to the bench next to me. Her thin, pale skin and lack of hair made her more skull than soldier.

"That's a good idea," she said, gesturing to how we'd laid out our uniforms. She rubbed at her newly shorn hair. "I'm Alsu Almas."

Masha and I told her our names, and while we were talking, a group of six women walked in and took the bench by the front door, their ages ranging from late teens to late twenties. They talked easily, calling out one another's last names without hesitation. They seemed to know one another already, and I was curious why such a big group might have enlisted together.

"They're from the Women's Rights Committee," Alsu said. "I was behind them in the line."

Masha laughed. "Did they get a group bonus?"

Alsu took a look at the women. "They're here to show that women can do all the same things a man can do."

"That's a weak reason to get yourself killed in battle," Masha muttered.

"I thought you were in favor of women's rights," I said in surprise. All through our childhood Masha had always stood up to the boys, daring them to race her, daring them to call her weak.

"I am, but this seems like a stupid way to advocate for suffrage. We shouldn't get the vote because we're as strong as men, but because we're as capable of rational thought as they are."

A moment later, Sergeant Bochkareva entered the barracks. For the first time, she wasn't flanked by male officers. This was the women's barracks, after all. She was as impressive now as she was in the morning, uniform spotless, shoulders squared. The only detail that betrayed the fact she'd been standing all day was a slight limp as she walked along the benches.

"This is your last night in skirts," she said. "Prepare yourselves, because when you wake up in the morning, you'll discover the world has gone hard. And if you're wondering why you have no beds, it's because you're being trained for war. When you're at the front, you won't find a bed. You have half as much time to prepare for the front as the men have, so we'll waste no time."

One of the women from the Women's Rights Committee, a woman with heavy bags under her eyes, gestured that she wanted to talk. Sergeant Bochkareva grunted her acquiescence.

"We would like to thank you for organizing this for us. It is a great thing for women to be allowed to prove they are as brave and strong as the men. Finally, they will see that we are equals, that we can both fight on the battlefield and retain our femininity, that we—"

Bochkareva cut her off. "If you're here only for women's rights, you'll be disappointed. The army already knows what women can do on the battlefield. There've been dozens of other women who have joined up with the men and fought just as bravely. We aren't here to prove an ideal, but to win a war. That is the only reason anyone should be standing in this room!"

"Yes, but surely it is good for all women to—"

Bochkareva didn't bother to respond. She continued walking down the line, studying each of us. The committee women's mouths hung open, and Masha snickered.

"Listen up," Bochkareva continued. "In the morning, I want you in your boots, trousers, and shirts. Put your civilian dresses away. Send them home. From the moment I wake you at dawn, you'll forget you're a woman." She paused long enough to eye the group from the Women's Rights Committee. "You're soldiers now, and that is all."

She marched out the door leaving a wake of startled women and girls behind her. No one moved for a moment, and then all of us moved at once, like ants in water. Quickly, I disrobed and folded my skirt for the last time, then set it in the bottom of my bag. I left out one set of uniforms and put the rest on top of my civilian clothes, then pulled out the square pieces of linen they'd issued us. With a grin, I laid them out on my cot.

"What are these?" Masha asked.

"Portyanki," I said.

"You're kidding," Masha said, frowning. When I shook my head, she lifted hers up into the air like little flags of surrender, then glanced down at her new boots. "They couldn't give us stockings?"

"These are easier to issue," I said.

"But not to wear."

"I know these," Alsu said. She slipped her shoes off, laid one of the square linens on her cot, and set her foot onto it. With deft fingers, she wrapped her feet, tucking the stray corners in. Within seconds, her foot was wrapped.

Masha's jaw dropped.

"You've done this before," I said to Alsu.

"Yes, it's more common where I'm from. We don't have stockings in all the shops."

"Do you have shops?" I asked, laughing.

She smirked. "Not like here."

"Don't they bunch up in your boots?" Masha asked, as she slipped her shoes off and tried to copy what Alsu had just done.

"It's not too difficult," Alsu said. "My little girls have done it since they were three. And if all the soldier men can do it . . ."

"Right," I said, taking off my own shoes and starting to wrap my feet as Maxim had shown me. "We're at least as clever as they are."

I snuggled into my single sheet and tried to find a comfortable position on my board. It was impossible. Resigned, I lay on my back and watched Masha wrapping the portyanki again. She was moving more slowly this time, methodically tucking the ends in.

"What are you doing?" I asked, gesturing at her feet.

"Practicing. If we're being woken up at four in the morning, I don't want to have to struggle with these while my hands are still asleep."

Alsu, on Masha's other side, chuckled. Then she sat up and gave us a salute. "Good night, new friends."

Once the lights were out and the whispering had faded word by word till there was nothing but a scratching of consonants on the edges of sleep, I opened my eyes to the darkness.

When I was twelve, I'd snuck into my brother's barracks

one night. He had been there only a week, a new officer-in-training in our father's regiment. I was hoping to convince him to come back home. While the men were snoring, I tiptoed over to my brother's bed. But as I approached, I found three other men surrounding him, their bodies bending and jerking while they pounded Maxim with stockings full of something heavy—sand, maybe. He lay curled in a ball, silent and still. Taking it.

On instinct, I grabbed a nearby broom and charged at them. I managed to hit one in the shoulders and knock another onto the floor before the third grabbed me from behind and squeezed the air out of my lungs. Even though we were darkened by shadows and flickering gaslight, what happened next was forever etched in my mind: Maxim got off his bed, took me out of the other man's arms, and slapped me across the face. His eyes were dark, swirling eddies of shame. When Maxim pointed at the door for me to leave, I ran.

Not a word had been spoken. The only real sounds were those made by the contact of sock-covered weights on Maxim's skin and the slap across my cheek. My hits with the broom had been as effective, and as loud, as a birch branch brushing at a windowpane.

The next day I received a letter from Maxim saying he had to let them hit him. Otherwise, they'd never accept him as an equal in the regiment, since our father was the commander. He had to prove he was one of them.

The day after that, I received another letter. It was from Ilya Yudenich. He had heard what had happened in the barracks and offered to teach me how to fight. He'd taught me how to march when I was little, so I knew I could take him at his word.

I ignored Maxim until Christmas, but I wrote Ilya back that day.

Lying in the dark amongst the women, I remembered exactly how I felt in my brother's barracks that night, aware that I didn't belong there, but determined to face whatever I found.

"Was she so beautiful, Papa?"

"Why do you ask?"

"Because you said men believe beautiful women, and they do stupid things for them."

"It doesn't matter if Olga was beautiful or not. She was powerful and wise."

10

MAY 29, 1917

"GET up! Get up and put your boots on! The Kaiser's men shoot at dawn!"

I bolted from the bed and started slipping on my trousers. Some had wisely slept in their clothes, and they were already slipping on their boots and hats. Envying them, I struggled with the buttons going up the front of my tunic.

"You have exactly five minutes to be outside in formation!" Bochkareva shouted. Then she was gone and I could nearly taste the panic in the air.

With a prayer for my brother, I cinched his left-behind belt around my waist. The trousers didn't fit right because they'd been made for men, but I was confident they'd stay up. I shoved my wrapped feet into the boots—hard, cold leather that would probably rip my feet to shreds before the end of the day. There was nothing to be done about that. I grabbed my cap and raced out of the room, Masha at my heels.

A slithering fog lay heavy on the courtyard, sucking the heat from our bones. My eyes were still dazed, and I rubbed at them as Masha and I ran to the other women and girls, trying to find a place to stand. They were lining up, but no one knew what they were doing. Now that we were all out in the open, all together, I could fully appreciate how many women made it through the night. There must have been a thousand women milling around and rubbing sleep from their eyes. A thousand women without any idea on how to get into formation.

They shuffled into four long rows, but their height was uneven and the rows were as straight as the path of a drunkard. I glanced at Sergeant Bochkareva and the other instructors, all men, and saw by their expressions that they had noticed this. Sergeant Bochkareva's eyebrow was raised expectantly, and I knew we only had a minute before she rained hell on us for our sloppy alignment. I'd seen it all before when I would hide in the corners of the Field of Mars and watch the men train.

This was my chance. If I was going to make my father proud, I couldn't just join the women's battalion. I needed to be a leader.

I stepped out from the group, terrified of what I was about to do even though someone needed to. I went to the front and turned to face the women.

"Soldiers!" I shouted, but my voice was hoarse and only the front row seemed to have noticed me. I tried again, pushing up from deep within my chest. "*Soldiers!* We need to organize our columns!"

There was some muttering, and I heard a few call out, "What'd she say?"

I cupped my hands over my mouth. "We need to line up by height!"

Now they were all looking at me. Some had taken me seriously and looked like they were waiting for instruction.

"If you're taller than the woman in front of you, tap her

and take her place." Amazingly, they did it. It took longer than it should have, and I knew we'd passed the five minutes we'd originally been given, but Sergeant Bochkareva was waiting it out. I glanced at her over my shoulder. She was watching me, but not with scorn. If anything, she looked pleased, so I faced the women again. "Now, turn to your right and look at the person in front of you. Tap her shoulder if you're taller and take her place!"

This time they were quicker. When that was all done, I had them turn back to me, and then I swiveled around like Ilya had taught me and gave Sergeant Bochkareva a salute.

"All present and accounted for, Sergeant." It was what the soldiers always said after they'd gotten their battalions in line.

"Is that so?" she asked. She marched up to me and stopped one pace away. "How can you be sure they're all present if you haven't called roll?"

I swallowed, and she winked.

"Well, shit. You got them in line, Pavlova. It looks like we'll get you all trained in time."

After she dismissed me, I ran to the back where I discovered a hole in the last line. There, I caught my breath and ran through what I'd just done. Although I'd been afraid, I had stood in front of a thousand people and told them what to do. And they had listened to me.

Someone started counting us, which seemed easier than calling roll, and I took stock of our surroundings. I now noticed the male officers who'd been tasked to train us.

I counted four of them. I wondered how many of them were happy to take on the challenge, and how many doubted what we could do. They stood at the edge of my vision, observing us with blank faces. One officer, the lieutenant, watched

Sergeant Bochkareva more than us, as if to ensure she did her job well.

When they finished counting, the men dispersed around us. One went to the front, saying something to Sergeant Bochkareva, and then turned to us. He spread his legs casually and stretched his neck in a slow, purposeful roll.

"At ease, recruits. I'm Sergeant Zapilov. I'm here to help train you. I don't want to make assumptions, but since you're women, I wonder if you can run very far." He was taunting us. If Maxim and Ilya were here, they would probably remind me that this was one way army officers motivated their recruits.

Slowly, the girl beside me pulled her ankle up behind her and stretched her leg. She seemed eager to be off and running. I caught her smiling at me, urging me to do the same.

One by one, the formation yielded as the women started to stretch. A few did the usual exercises school children perform at the start of the day, reaching for their toes and then up at the bright blue sky.

After a minute, Zapilov gave us a nod. "Run behind me."

He turned and jogged away, kicking up flecks of gravel that skittered across the courtyard and hit the toes of the first line of women. Sergeant Bochkareva was at the side now, shouting for us to move. Like an accordion pulling apart to breathe, we staggered forward and ran after Zapilov. I quickly spotted Masha bobbing amongst the women in front.

The girl beside me sprang from each step easy as a deer, even though her new boots clomped and she had to pull up her trousers every few steps. While we ran, the wool of my too-large trousers rubbed together and we hadn't made it once around the courtyard before it started to chafe.

"Catch up to the front!" Sergeant Bochkareva yelled at a

handful of women in the middle who'd slowed down. Sergeant Zapilov was taking us in a circuit within the courtyard without so much as a glance at the gates that led out into the city proper. "Running together will keep us alive. If you strike off alone, you're an easier target! Always stick together."

The women in the middle sped up, but Bochkareva wasn't done with us. "Take a look behind you. If you're too far ahead, make adjustments. We are a battalion, not a herd of reindeer!"

I snorted at this because I'd heard it before. When I trained with Ilya, he'd made me run behind the other formations. I was never allowed within their ranks, but I was close enough to hear the sergeants shouting insults and motivational quips. I heard their songs, their shouts of triumph, and their groans. What we needed now was a song to keep us together, but I was not going to volunteer for that.

"You know what you're doing," remarked the girl soldier next to me. She wasn't breathing heavily at all.

"I used to run a lot."

"I don't think anyone else knows how."

We circled the courtyard two more times before Sergeant Zapilov slowed us down to a walk. He turned to face us, walking backwards now, and took stock. We had thinned out. A least fifty women had fallen out and were walking gingerly along the edge of our circuit.

"You'll have to do better than that next time," he said.

His voice echoed off the buildings: *next time, next time, next time.*

I nodded as if he'd spoken to me in particular. There was a blister forming on my heel, and it burned, but I couldn't let it slow me down.

Once the other women rejoined the ranks, we were escorted to the dining hall for kasha and cream, smoked salmon as thin as tissue paper, and steaming cups of tea. It was gone within minutes, and the women who'd started the meal with delicacy were now scrambling to get the last bites off the tables. No one was sure when we'd eat next, or what they'd have us do now. The threat of the unknown stripped away any inhibitions. With so many women grabbing for the last spoonful of kasha, there was no room for table manners.

"I'm training soldiers, not pigs!" Sergeant Bochkareva snapped. "You'll get fed enough, don't fight over it."

Over the next several hours, we learned how to march, how to walk in formation, and how to swing our arms. By midday, we began to feel less like a collection of stray cats, but we were still an unimpressive sight.

After our midday meal, a woman behind me voiced what many of us must have been thinking. "If we march like this in battle, we'll have no chance of winning the war."

Sergeant Bochkareva's lips pressed into a thin, white line, as though she was doing her best to keep certain words from exploding out of her mouth. Then, with a sharp glance at the perpetrator, she called for the battalion to halt.

"Trust that I am training you quickly and thoroughly for the front. Learning how to march is what teaches you how to listen to one another's movements. It's how you become a unit. We won't fight this way. Tomorrow, we learn how to do that."

She said something to one of the trainers, and then marched ahead to another group of recruits. It wasn't long before we could hear her shouts across the courtyard, cutting into someone for turning left when everyone else turned right.

That night we fell onto our boards, exhausted. Masha sewed the chevrons onto our extra tunics while I took care of our boots, buffing the dirt off them. When she wasn't looking, I took stock of my right heel. The skin had slid off and was stuck in the weave of my portyanki. Gingerly, I pulled off the extra skin. The blister had come and gone, but now I was left with a bright pink hole in my skin. As smoothly as I could, I rewrapped the linen portyanki around my foot, making sure to add extra padding at the heel.

I had it all done before Masha finished stitching up the last of the chevrons. She was doing Alsu's now and had one of the pins stuck between her lips, her brow furrowed in concentration. Even with her hair shorn off, with the pin stuck there and her lips pursed, she looked like a girl fixing her brother's uniform before he ran off to play soldier.

I stretched my legs out on the board. "Anything else we need to do?"

Alsu huffed. "We could eat again."

Masha tossed the tunic at Alsu, who caught it in the air. "I am dead. My body aches so much I can hardly move. And these boards! How does she expect us to get any sleep? I think the floor would be more comfortable."

"Except for the rats," I said. No one laughed.

We hadn't been issued nightclothes, so we kept our tunics and trousers on, tucking our greatcoats beneath us as pillows. I looked around and saw that everyone was doing the same, some lying on top of the sheet and some wrapping themselves in it like swaddling clothes, but all of us kept our uniforms on.

"If you can't sleep, I can tell you a Tatar bedtime story," said Alsu. Masha snorted, and Alsu rolled onto her side, facing the two of us. "It works on my daughters. Should work on you two."

"Goodnight, Mama Alsu," I said and laid my forearm over my eyes to block out the late-night sun peeking through the curtains. One of the women had pulled the curtains shut, but the light broke through anyway, scattering across the women in sharp stripes.

That night, I barely thought of Maxim or my father. I could barely think of the war itself. My mind grew sluggish, my body heavy, and I was out before my fears could find me.

"Olga had her people refrain from drinking the mead they'd brought, and when Prince Mal's men were drunk, her people killed them all."

"All of them? There weren't any who snuck away?"

"They say five thousand people were massacred."

"This is a really awful bedtime story, Papa."

11

JUNE 3, 1917

THERE was no time to rest or heal when you were training to be a soldier. My nose was four inches from the dirt and my arms were shaking as they tried to hold me up. My body screamed, but I would not allow myself to rest on the ground.

One of the instructors stepped closer and crouched beside me. The gravel and dirt scraped beneath him as he bent down.

"Your back isn't straight."

It was Sergeant Brusilov, one of the quieter instructors. He rarely spoke, but when he did the words went straight to your bones. This time, his voice somehow filtered through my body's agony and I pulled my stomach tighter. My back straightened.

"Yes," he said, and then he was gone.

I grunted and was echoed by hundreds of other women as we all fought to keep ourselves off the ground. I heard a collapse followed by a groan of disappointment, but most of us managed.

"Thirty-eight!" Sergeant Bochkareva called out. I popped my arms up until they were straight and allowed my knees to bend a little, relieving the strain on my lower back. Now that I was up off the ground, I could look around. Little more than half of us were left. As we fell, the trainers brought us out of formation and lined us up against the wall. The expressions of the women there were a mixture of relief and embarrassment.

I had done push-ups before, but Sergeant Bochkareva twisted this into a game of agony, in which we felt every muscle, from our ears down to our toes, burning.

"Down!" she ordered. I sank, tightening my muscles in my stomach so that I didn't collapse. My ears were ringing, but I could still hear her. "One of the hardest things we had to put up with at the front was muscle fatigue. When you carry your kit for days, marching over fields of mud and ice, you will get tired. Your body will say 'This is enough!'" She paused. "Thirty-nine."

I pushed up. The woman next to me didn't get up. Her elbows wobbled a moment before she sank. She moaned in relief, lying flat on her stomach, until Sergeant Brusilov tapped her shoulder.

Sergeant Bochkareva paced before us. Her eyes flickered toward the women walking away. "It is only pain, and it will be gone as soon as you quit. But you cannot quit yet. Your body must be trained to endure fatigue. You must be able to carry your own weight, your own kit, and your own rifle. Just like the men. Down!"

I could not do this any longer. My arms felt as though they were ripping apart, and my back was a rack of pain. Sergeant Bochkareva's voice carried across the field.

"You must be strong! Most men can do fifty push-ups, easily. Forty!"

I tried to push my body up, but my arms had nothing left to burn. I made it halfway before I fell and my face hit the dirt. Sergeant Brusilov tapped my shoulder almost instantly. He must have known it was my time and had been hovering there, waiting. I crawled up to my knees, brushed the dirt off my face, and watched the rest of the women continue. Sergeant Brusilov pointed to the wall, and if my face wasn't already red with exhaustion it would redden now with shame.

"You had thirty-nine," he said. "A good number."

I nodded, more to acknowledge him than to agree. If most men could do fifty, then thirty-nine wasn't anything to crow over. I stepped over the legs of the others and reached the wall, where I sat and tucked my knees up to my chest. There, while my body buzzed with the sudden absence of torture, I watched the remainder. How could they push on? How were they not as expired as I?

"We were in retreat," Bochkareva continued her tale. "We'd been fighting for most of the day when the call was made. Half my platoon lay flat out in the mud, and as I ran to the back, I heard them calling to me." She cleared her throat and circled the remaining recruits. "Down."

The women went down, and I watched as exhaustion took them like a disease. Ten more surrendered and were herded over to where I sat, each of them one push-up stronger than me. "I couldn't run back and ignore them! So I picked up my nearest comrade and carried him on my shoulder while the Germans shot at me from behind. Forty-one!"

The women grunted and groaned, but they pushed their shoulders and hips up off the ground.

Bochkareva stopped pacing. "I went back and got as many as I could, and each step I took could have been my last. I was

108

afraid and my body screamed at me to stop. It was too hard. They were too heavy, and I had been fighting for too long. I needed to rest." She pounded her chest with a fist. "But I could not let them die just because I was tired!"

Shame crawled along the wall as slick as a serpent, and those of us who felt it shifted on the balls of our feet. The knowledge that I might fail, that I might be too petrified to help when my sisters-in-arms needed me most coiled in my stomach. The recruit beside me, a girl about my age named Kosik, shrugged ever so slightly.

"I wasn't just tired," she whispered. "I couldn't do it any longer. My arms didn't *work*."

I squeezed the muscles of my upper arms. I wanted to agree with her. I wanted to say that I'd pushed my body as far as it could go, but there had been a moment when I made the decision to quit. It had been a choice. "I could have." I looked away, but not before catching the doubt in her watery-blue eyes.

"When the time comes, you'll be strong enough," she said.

I thought of the day the Cossacks charged us in the street, when everyone thought I was standing tall and brave, but I had instead been frozen in fear. When we were at the front and the moment of truth came, would I be a Valkyrie running at the enemy, or would I stand frozen in the mud, my heart in my mouth, unable to breathe?

I slumped deeper into the wall, keeping an eye on Sergeant Brusilov. He escorted half a dozen women, and only three remained on the ground. One was Korlova, a Ukrainian woman who'd shown incredible strength. One was Muravyeva, a young woman with a fierce curl to her lips. Her body shook with the stress she was putting on it, but she did not give up. The third woman was Dubrovskaya, the girl I'd run with on our first day of training. She didn't have an ounce of fat on her, and despite her frail frame, was able to hold her body low to the ground without any obvious strain. She must have grown up in the circus.

Sergeant Bochkareva stopped in front of Muravyeva. "These women will be the ones to save you. Trust in their strength." Then she crouched down between them. "Get up."

The three rose from the ground, moving slowly. They'd pushed themselves as far as they could go. Unlike me, they hadn't given up. It showed in their determined, dazed faces.

Dubrovskaya caught my eyes and smiled, weakly. It stabbed at me. I'd disappointed her.

JUNE 8, 1917

I woke up gulping for air, and my heart raced as if I'd been sprinting. The room was still and silent but for a few snores and the rapid beating of my heart. As quietly as I could, I pulled the blanket back and let the heat steam off my stomach and my legs. Then I noticed the draft.

The window was open.

Someone had propped it ajar with a can of shoe polish. It was only a crack, but it was enough to let the wind in and rustle the curtain. Filtered light slithered across the room and draped over the ends of my toes, leaving pockets of shadow in the blanket folds.

I groaned, because if we left it open all night, we'd be covered in dew by morning. With aching muscles, I rolled off the bench and headed for the window. There was an empty spot where a uniform factory girl usually slept. She was either in the toilet or had gone out the window, because there was no trace of her in the room. I would've spotted her white-blonde hair glowing like a lantern.

Slowly, I pulled back the curtain and looked out onto the street. A few people stumbled along the sidewalk, propping each other up. There was no trace of the missing girl, but across the street and plastered to a boarded-up window was a sign that set my heart to racing again.

It was just a little red star above the stenciled words "Carry for the People." To anyone else in the barracks, it was just an annoying sign the socialists probably put up. To me, it was a call.

I gripped the windowsill and cursed the stars above. I knew they were there, even if I couldn't see them through the haze of streetlights and summer dusk. I'd left that world, but it had followed me here.

Maybe it was a coincidence. Maybe the sign was there for someone else. I couldn't be the only friend of the Bolsheviks in the battalion. But even as I tried to deny it, I knew it was for me.

I wouldn't go. It didn't matter if Sergei himself serenaded me from the street below. I was in the army now. Whatever he needed, he could get it somewhere else. Plenty of other girls had useful social connections he could use to his advantage.

Before I realized what I was doing, I was tying on my boots.

I slid the window up high enough to slip out, climbed down using the mortar between the bricks as footholds, and jumped the last meter to the ground. My entire body felt like I'd been run over by a trolley, but it was just sore muscles from the day's training.

I landed softly in the dirt behind a rose bush and took a moment to check I hadn't left a trail of footprints on the wall. The light was fading, but only because the sun was behind the building. The street was cast in shadow, and the edges were soft in that tricky way dusk has of making us believe we're walking through a veil. The single streetlamp lit the corner like a spot onstage.

With another look at the red star, I walked briskly down the sidewalk, taking on a man's gait and keeping to the darkest patches. My uniform would draw attention, as would my lack of comrades-in-arms. And then, naturally, anyone would notice I was not a man if they looked closely enough.

There was a crack in the shadows, and I jumped.

Sergei stepped up from behind a cart. His eyes blinked at me, catching the last glimmer of light. They were the only things about him that I could differentiate from the surrounding shadow.

"You came." His voice was gruffer than usual.

"I shouldn't have."

I ground my boots into the dirt and watched him, waiting for him to make the first move. After a moment, he sighed and came closer. He smelled of tea and printers' ink, and the scent whirled around me, teasing me with the life I used to live.

"You've cut your hair," I said. It was shorn close on the sides, but was longer on top than mine.

"As have you."

I rubbed at the back of my head and felt the hairs prickle my palm. "It's the latest fashion."

He didn't laugh. Instead, he shoved his fists into his pockets, as though he was afraid to touch me. "I have to tell you something."

"What?"

"My comrades haven't forgotten you. They've found out where you are now and what you're doing."

"I wonder how," I said dryly, though he looked offended that I would suspect him. "Why do they care? I was just a courier."

"No, you weren't. You were an informant."

"One of hundreds, I'm sure. And I'm finished now."

He shook his head. "I've been asked to talk to you, on behalf of the party leadership."

"If this is going to be another lecture about the senseless-ness of contributing to the war effort—"

Sergei cut me off. "The battalion can't go to the front. It needs to fail, Katya. We need you to make certain it fails."

"So they're asking for sabotage." I crossed my arms. "I can't do that."

"It has to be done."

I held his gaze. "I owe the Bolsheviks nothing."

"The revolution is bigger than either of us, Katya. You can't deny that the world is changing. Don't you want it to go in the right direction?"

"Yes. But I can't sabotage my battalion!"

His eyes widened. "Keep your voice down."

I glared at him. "The Bolsheviks will have to find some other way to end the war." I turned to go, but Sergei moved to stand in front of me.

"Look, all you have to do is find a way to keep the women off the train. You can stay here as a battalion. You can be 'protectors of Petrograd' if you like. Just don't go to the front."

"Get out of my way, Sergei Fyodorovich."

"If you keep the women's battalion in Petrograd, you'll be saving lives. Not just the lives of these women, but of anyone who might die if this hopeless war drags on.'"

"What about the lives that have already been spent?" I nearly spat the words out.

"We can't do anything about that past. All we can do is shape the future."

"It isn't hopeless. I'm betting my life on it."

"I pray you're right, because you're betting more than just your own life."

His words followed me all the way back to the barracks and wrapped around me tighter than my portyanki. They strangled me till dawn.

———

JUNE 10, 1917

Lieutenant Ornilov took us to the armory to retrieve our weapons. After lining us up outside the building, he called us in, column by column. I was one of the first to enter. A sergeant with a mustache that more than made up for his stature nodded his head at Lieutenant Ornilov.

"Ready, are they?" he asked.

"They don't have the time not to be," growled Ornilov.

Inside, we were enveloped by a cool, dark interior. It smelled of iron, candle wax, and grease. I had always imagined the armory to be divided into rooms, like the cells of a prison, but instead of prisoners each cell would be stocked with a particular type of weapon. There would be a cell with rifles, one for grenades, one for knives . . .

But this was nothing like I'd imagined. It was a great open hall lined with shelves. The weapons were piled or stacked according to type, and in the back corner was a smaller door, made of steel, with a sign declaring it full of explosive powder. My fingers, still yellowed from the TNT, itched whenever I looked at that door.

The sergeant went to a wide rack against the back wall and gestured at a collection of rifles. "Take one and go to the table over there. Write down its serial number in the book and get back outside."

The rifles were filthy, coated in dried mud. The bayonets were still attached, but not all of them were complete. The leather straps were cracked, and some had broken buckles.

I glanced back at the sergeant. "Are these—"

"I said grab one and go sign the book!" He pulled at his mustache. "I know they're a disaster, but this is all we've got. You should be glad you're getting any weapon at all. The last platoon had to go on without!"

I fingered the rifles. Beneath the first layer, I found one without too much dirt or rust, and it had all its components. I picked it up while the women behind me swarmed at the remaining rifles.

"You know what they were told?" he asked me.

"No, sergeant." I paused on my way to the logbook.

"They were told to pick a rifle off the first dead soldier they come across, Russian or German. We don't have any more to hand out." He laughed. "But of course we had some set aside for the *women*."

I rushed to the table, found the book and pencil, and signed my name. It took me a moment to pinpoint where the serial number was inscribed, but I found it on the receiver, near the bolt: 703552. I scratched it into the logbook and stepped aside so the woman behind me could do the same. She took a while to find the serial number, so I ended up showing everyone where it was located. One of the recruits had to scrape away a thick coating of grease with her thumbnail. When we were finished, I led them back out into the sun.

It was another hour before we'd each received a weapon and been taught how to carry it on our shoulders while marching. The rifle was heavier than I'd expected, and it slipped in my hand a few times when I went to raise it onto my shoulder. Some of the women dropped theirs and were met with shouts from the sergeant.

"Don't drop my weapons! As dirty as they are now, they're good enough for battle. Get them clean and keep them that way. Think of them as you would a baby. Hell, some of you have babies somewhere, so you know what it's like. These are cavalry rifles, chosen for you because they're two kilos lighter than the regular M-91s. Your rifle is your weapon and your shield. Keep it clean, don't drop it, and bring it back in one piece." Then he saluted Lieutenant Ornilov and slunk back into his armory.

When he was gone, the lieutenant snapped around to face us. He called us to attention and shouted, "Right shoulder, arms!"

It was a mess. We weren't in unison, and someone nearly dropped her rifle, but eventually we got them in the right place.

JUNE 14, 1917

"Recruit Pavlova," Sergeant Bochkareva said. We were in a classroom with our rifles spread across the desks before us, and Sergeant Bochkareva had been going over the parts of the rifle.

I glanced up. "Yes, Sergeant?"

"What is the serial number of your piece?" I peered at my bolt, but her hand reached out and covered it. "You should have memorized it by now."

"I only looked at it twice." Memorizing random numbers was not one of my greater talents.

"Then you should pay more attention to the lesson than to that blank space on the table. And for the rest of you, it is important that you know those numbers by heart, because in the heat of battle, you'll want to make sure you have your own rifle in your hands. A poorly kept rifle could backfire in your face. You can't trust any but your own." She paused and licked her thumb, which she then used to wipe the dirt off the inscription on my receiver. I stared at the spit-cleaned numbers, now shiny, trying to brand them into my brain.

703552.

I would never forget again.

Sergeant Bochkareva held up a bucket full of leather bags. "These are your rifle kits. I had them brought over this morning from the armory." One of the recruits walked around with the bucket and tossed each of us one of the kit bags. They landed with a dull thud.

Some of the women were picking at their weapons, scratching at the wooden stock with delicate, light strokes. One recruit looked like she was afraid to touch it or it'd go off. I slid open the latch of the steel plate on the buttstock and reached inside to find the cleaning rod. I pulled it out, screwed the separate pieces together, and then opened the kit bag to take out the oil bottle and a rag.

The bottle was flat and round, and the inside was divided into two compartments with separate screw-on caps. One side of the bottle held the cleaning solution, and the other held oil. As a child, I used to play with bottles like these. We kept a few in the kitchen, until I tried to convince my mother that we could use them for the oil and vinegar; the next day, they were gone.

With a click and a tug, I removed the bolt and firing chamber and laid them on the table. Then I pulled the band off the stock and removed it. The barrel wasn't as dirty as I'd feared, and there were no signs of rust. The stock fell off easily in my hands. Now that the large pieces were taken apart, I started to dismantle the bolt and firing chamber. It was tricky, because there were tiny pieces, including a spring with a tendency to bounce away. I'd once lost Maxim's spring in the carpet, and it'd taken me the better part of an hour to find it again.

I was in the middle of wiping the smaller parts with the rag when I felt a weight on my shoulder. It was Sergeant Bochkareva. Most of her bulk loomed over the space between Masha and me.

"When you've finished, help your friend." She stepped back, and Masha smirked.

"Yes, well done, Pavlova." Masha tugged at the latch on the butt plate. "I'm not so sure being raised by academics will take me far in this war."

"At least you can read," Bochkareva said flatly. Then she was moving on, helping the others.

Masha leaned closer. "She can't read?" she whispered.

I watched Bochkareva show Lomonosova how to pull the bolt back. "I don't know. I bet half the women here can't."

Masha frowned while pulling the cleaning rod out. "I forget

118

sometimes." She snapped the cleaning rod together as though she'd done it before, and I raised my brows in approval.

"Well, Gubina," I said, using Masha's surname like she'd used mine, "it's time you learn how to properly clean your rifle, because my life might depend on it."

She rolled her eyes, but for the next half hour, she listened intently to everything I said. When we were done, the room was divided into two groups, one with Bochkareva and the rest leaning over my desk. Each of us taught the others everything they needed to know about the rifle. Other than how to kill with it, of course.

When we were done, the rifles were in marginally better shape. Mine was gleaming, even the chipped parts. I ran my fingers gently along the stock, which was slick from oil. The bolt slid out easily, and when I held the barrel up to the light of the window, it was clear of any dust.

"Let me check," Bochkareva said. I gave her my rifle, and she peered from where the bolt goes in up the length of the barrel. I watch her mouth, which tightened. With a sniff, she handed the rifle back to me. "Good. You did well teaching the others."

Masha mouthed "Good job, Pavlova," and I swallowed back a grin. I ignored everyone's comments and gave Bochkareva a quick nod before packing up my kit. When we were dismissed a moment later to return to our barracks, Bochkareva stopped me at the door. Masha gestured silently that she'd see me at the barracks, but her eyes were full of curiosity. She'd be waiting impatiently to hear what Bochkareva said to me.

"Sergeant." I stood at attention.

Her eyes were surprisingly soft. "Pavlova, do you know how many women are still here to train?"

"Five hundred?"

She shook her head. "Three hundred and thirty-four. We started off with two thousand, and we'll probably lose a few more before we head to the front." My fingers stung from the cleaning solution, and I squeezed my fists. "You've done well, and I have no doubt you'll be one of them."

"Thank you, Sergeant."

"Tonight I'm organizing the battalion into four platoons. I want you to lead one of them."

I had hoped for this kind of recognition, this kind of chance to stand out among my fellow recruits. And yet, the weight of it settled onto my shoulders like an itchy blanket. Being platoon leader would mean more stress and less peace of mind.

"You've grown up in this life and your experience can benefit these women. We only have a few more weeks until we have to be ready to fight. If I don't get help from those who already know what they're doing, none of us will make it on that train."

The image of Maxim through the train window, waving at me just before he slipped out the back compartment, came to the front of my mind.

"I'm not *asking* you to lead the platoon, Pavlova."

"Yes, Sergeant. Understood."

Although she hadn't given me any choice in the matter, she looked relieved. "When you get your list of women in your platoon, it'll be your responsibility to help train them. Their lives will depend on you. They'll be yours."

"Yes, Sergeant."

"I won't be running this battalion on a committee, like the socialists want us to. Some women will want to discuss our maneuvers like we're planning a party. But this is war, and my orders will be your life. What *I* say is the law."

I knew what she was getting at. "You want me to ensure the women in my platoon obey you, no matter what."

"We will be an exemplary battalion. One the army has never seen before. We have to be strong. We have to be better than the men."

I saluted her and stepped outside with my rifle slung over my shoulder.

"Finally, Prince Mal realized he needed to apologize for having Igor killed, so he sent another tribute to Olga, who had returned to Kiev."

"How did he not die in the massacre?"

"I—he wasn't there."

"And he still had enough people to deliver this tribute? What was it?"

"Honey and furs, usually."

"I want a tribute."

"I'm about to switch over to Saint Kirill."

12

JUNE 15, 1917

BOCHKAREVA began the next phase after breakfast. Without any explanation, she began calling out names, firing them off one after the other. After she'd called out about fifty, she said, "You are the First Platoon. Form up over there," and she pointed to an area off to her right.

Soon everyone would know I'd been assigned as the leader of one of these new platoons. I tried to catch Masha's eyes, but she was watching Bochkareva with an intent look on her face.

Bochkareva called out another set of names and declared them to be the second platoon. Masha and Alsu had not yet been called, and the odds were growing greater that they'd be together.

I desperately hoped Masha would be in my platoon. I didn't want her to be in another platoon where I couldn't keep an eye on her. If we were separated, we wouldn't be able to talk as much, and I'd be truly alone amongst all these women.

Bochkareva's voice carried out across the yard, assigning Masha and Alsu to the same platoon. When my name wasn't called, Masha finally turned to me, frowning, about to ask a question.

Bochkareva's voice rang out: "Third Platoon, get in formation over by the fence!"

"You'd better go," I said. I tried to smile, sure that unease was painted across my face.

Bochkareva called out the fourth platoon, sent them over to the only remaining spot, and then turned to the four of us who remained.

"Avilova, you take the first platoon. Liddikova, the second. Pavlova, you get the third and Mussorgskaya, you have the fourth. Get your women in line and then take them to your next training activity. I'll have the training officers let you know where you're to go next."

Masha and Alsu were in my platoon. I tried not to smile too wide as I marched over to the group of women getting themselves into formation. Considering they'd only learned how to march a few weeks ago, they weren't doing too badly. Fifty-five women, most of them a few years older than me. At least five were closer to thirty. And all of them would want to know why a seventeen-year-old factory worker was chosen to lead them.

I stopped and snapped my heels together.

"Third Platoon!" I said. "I'm Ekaterina Viktorovna Pavlova, your platoon leader."

Surprise and uncertainty crawled through the silence. One of the women—Muravyeva, who had the shiniest boots in Petrograd and was best at push-ups—pursed her lips in distaste. Either she had expected to be a platoon leader herself, or she simply didn't like having me in charge.

A moment later, Lieutenant Ornilov came up to us carrying a rifle. I brought the platoon to attention and saluted him. He waved us back at ease.

"Congratulations on your promotion, Pavlova."

"Thank you, sir."

"I'm here to take you to your next training exercise." He lifted the rifle up before the platoon. "We'll be doing some hand-to-hand fighting, but with rifles. Grab your weapons and meet me on the grass in ten minutes."

I nodded, saluted again, and ordered the platoon to get their weapons.

They were halfway to the barracks before I remembered I hadn't told them to form up outside. Hoping they'd be smart enough to figure that one out for themselves, I caught up with Masha and Alsu, who'd held back before going inside the building.

"Congratulations, Katya," Alsu said. Her eyes crinkled as she smiled.

"Thank you."

"You knew, didn't you?" Masha said, smacking my shoulder. "Why didn't you tell us?"

"I only found out last night, and I didn't know who would get assigned to my platoon."

After a giant, dramatic sigh, Masha added, "I suppose now we'll have to do everything you say."

"Of course."

She smacked me again. "Don't push it, Pavlova. Just because your father is so high up . . ."

"That's not it," I blurted, hurt that Masha would even suggest it. "I mean, Sergeant Bochkareva didn't choose me because of his rank. But because I know some things about the army already."

"All you knew how to do was march. And we've learned that."

Her tone was like a shard of ice poking into my chest. "Do you not want to be in my platoon?"

"Of course I do. You think I want to be with Avilova and march to suffragette songs?" She gave me a one-armed hug. "I just hope you know what you're doing."

I pulled out of her embrace, trying not to look offended. "Better get your rifles. We'll form up out here and march to the green," I said, loud enough for most of the women to hear me.

The blonde Avilova was already gathering her platoon on the other side of the courtyard. I suspected she'd been given a command position due to her influence on a large portion of the battalion who'd joined in the name of women's rights. Instead of alienating them, Bochkareva had done the smart thing and given them their own platoon. Avilova's sharp features matched the pitch of her voice, and her soldiers seemed to snap together nicely. Quicker than mine did.

I managed to march my platoon to the green without incident, thankful every step of the way for my childhood training. Lieutenant Ornilov brought us into three lines and showed us how to use the rifle in close quarters. We jabbed in the air with our bayonets, we blocked invisible opponents with the rifle stock, and we smashed in imaginary heads with the butt of the rifle.

After half an hour of this, I could barely lift my rifle higher than my waist without wincing. I had to look competent despite the burning in my arms, so I kept my face as expressionless as I could.

"Now, pair off," Lieutenant Ornilov said, stepping back.

The women started finding partners. Masha and Alsu paired with each other, and after a moment, everyone stood facing another soldier. All except for Muravyeva, who stood off to the side, rifle on one shoulder and a hand on her other hip.

I looked to Lieutenant Ornilov, and he cocked a brow. *Go on*, he seemed to say, *it's your platoon*.

"You'll be my partner," I told her.

Lieutenant Ornilov came over to us. "Try to get your partner to the ground," he said, speaking to the group at large but looking at me. "Don't worry about bruises. They'll fade."

Muravyeva brought her rifle down to where it crossed over her chest, bayonet pointing and glinting at the sun.

"Normally, we have the men take the bayonets off for this first exercise," Lieutenant Ornilov said. "But you have a shorter training schedule. Can I trust you not to impale one another?"

There were a few chuckles. Muravyeva looked directly into my eyes, unblinking.

"Don't worry," she said. She flashed her teeth. "I won't stab you."

I smiled back. "I'm not worried. Have you ever done this before?"

"No, but I grew up with six older brothers who knew how to use sticks. Sharp ones."

Lieutenant Ornilov looked me up and down, eyes criticizing my stance and my grip, then gestured at Muravyeva. "Why don't you show your platoon what to do, Pavlova?"

"Yes, sir." I took a step back from Muravyeva and held the rifle in front of me, opposite hers. She stood a few inches shorter than me, but her stance showed confidence.

I cocked my chin at her. "All right then. Let's do this."

The other women shifted their stances to get a clearer look at us. I knew many of them would judge me based on how well I fought.

Muravyeva charged without warning, without wrinkling

her brow, and slammed her rifle into mine. The rifles clapped together, and her rifle butt smashed my fingers. I almost let go, shocked at the pulsing sting coming from my fingers. Grimacing, I pushed my weight into her, trying to get a grip on the slippery grass.

When she slid a bit, I took a step back and let her fall forward, then jammed my rifle butt into her shoulder. She cried out but didn't fall. Her face flushed red and her eyes became fierce coals. She kicked out, slicing the toe of her boot at my knee. I grunted at the pain, but I couldn't stop. I couldn't fall.

I pulled back, bringing the rifle with me, then with a sharp twist, smashed the entire rifle into her chest, crushing her fingers and knocking her to the ground. Before she could scramble back up, I turned the rifle on her, pointing the bayonet at her throat.

With a grunt, she swept her boot up and around and kicked my rifle. It flew, strap flapping, and clattered to the ground. I leapt for it, but I wasn't fast enough to avoid the stock of her rifle. She slammed it into the side of my head and I toppled over. My face hit the dirt and my cheek crackled in pain. The world erupted in red and black bursts, and behind me I heard a whoop of victory.

She had won.

I took a moment to catch my breath and settle my head before sliding up onto my knees.

Muravyeva wiped at the sweat on her forehead, leaving a streak of grime over one eye like a second eyebrow. Then she pulled me off the ground and clutched my wrist. The scorn she'd worn earlier had been replaced by shadows.

"How many brothers went to fight?" I asked.

"All of them."

The air between us blew cold, wrapping around my ankles. "And . . ." I trailed off, not actually wanting to know.

She hoisted her rifle over her shoulder. "All but one are dead." Then she stalked over to the rest of the platoon and fell into a position at the end of the line.

"Well done, both of you," Lieutenant Ornilov said. "Let's get the rest of the platoon fighting like you two."

Between us, Muravyeva and I managed to get the platoon comfortable with the idea of smashing one another with rifles, and we only had to send three women to the infirmary for injuries. The rest of us wiped ourselves off.

Though Muravyeva had bested me, I felt I'd acquitted myself well in front of my platoon. I could do this. I could lead these women. As long as I didn't freeze up when we were being shot at.

JUNE 16, 1917

We were marching through a thin blanket of fog to the Field of Mars, where the grass had given way to mud. When the army had brought in truckloads of sand to level and dry it out, the soldiers had begun calling it the Sahara. Today, where men had trained for generations, we marched in lines and columns until every single woman knew her leader's command almost before it was spoken. Exhilaration rushed through me. The platoon was beginning to feel like it was *mine*.

Once we'd satisfied the trainers and it was time to return to the barracks, Masha ran up to me and slapped me on the back. "That was good! We're getting good at this!" she said giddily.

I grinned at her. "We're going to be terrifying on the

battlefield, Masha. The Germans will run screaming back to the Rhine."

As Masha turned to talk to Alsu, Avilova marched her platoon past mine and gave me a mocking salute. She paused next to me, letting her soldiers walk on.

"You need to be careful about favoritism, Pavlova." She looked pointedly at Masha.

"I'm not—"

She raised her hand up to shush me, then turned to walk backwards with the last of her platoon. "You need to lead them. Don't be stupid."

Then she turned back around and said something to the last woman in her platoon, who laughed. I knew it couldn't have been about me, but I still felt like they were laughing at me.

I got my women back in line and into a march, but my mind was on Avilova. Masha was my best friend and I spoke with her more than with anyone else, but I didn't make her life any easier. I expected the same from her that I expected from the others. And she knew it, surely.

My soldiers kept in step the whole way back to the barracks, not breaking formation until they'd been told to fall out and go inside to wash up. Masha and Alsu waited for me, both of them gripping the rifle slings that hung over their shoulders.

"What'd Avilova say to you?" asked Alsu.

"That I need to step up as a leader." It wasn't a lie.

Later that day, we were taken out of the city for target practice at the seashore. The winds racing off the Baltic smelled of salt and saltpeter.

Our targets were fifty meters away. I lay on my stomach in the sand, propped my elbows up, pulled the bolt back, and opened the receiver. One bullet. We each had three, and we had to hit the target with at least one of them. I inserted the first bullet, felt it catch, and slid the bolt closed. It clicked.

I took aim, running my eyes down the stock and leveling the rifle so the target appeared directly in the little valley of the metal piece at the end. I took a deep breath, exhaled, and then squeezed the trigger.

Bam! The force jammed the stock into my shoulder, but I'd had lots of practice recently and the bruising there had turned hard. I barely noticed the pressure anymore.

I blinked, looked down the range, and saw that I had nicked the outer ring. Our shots had to be inside the ring to count. With a quiet curse, I reloaded. As I did so, I looked at the other recruits. Masha was two people down from me, loading her third shot. Alsu had already done this test and had moved on to the next one.

Again, I aimed. This time, I waited for the wind to die down and then pulled the trigger. The rifle hit me in the shoulder, and the bullet tore through the edge of the target again. I had one more bullet left.

The third time, I hit inside the outer ring.

"You'll have to do better if you want your platoon to follow you in battle." Bochkareva's deep voice rumbled over my shoulder blades.

"Yes, Sergeant."

Next came throwing grenades, and this I enjoyed more. I was good at it. Better than I'd been at filling them, even. The first time we'd come to the beach and thrown dummy grenades at barrels, I let the handle roll off my finger and it flew end over end and hit the outlined spot in the dirt. Every single barrel I aimed at, I dented. I could throw them twenty, thirty meters with accuracy. As children, Maxim and I had thrown rocks at the Neva, skipping them over the surface till they plunked into the water. There was a trick to it, letting the smooth stone slide over your fingers, slipping just so. In my fingers the grenade became a stone, the land between me and the barrel a river. And Maxim's laughter echoed in my ears.

When we finished with the dummies, our trainers led us to the dunes. Dozens of metal crates lined up along one edge of the field, dull gray in the cloud-covered sky. Masha sucked in her breath, and I grimaced. These were crates she had packed. They were from our factory.

Sergeant Zapilov stood in front of the crates, his legs spread wide and his arms crossed in front of him. He scowled, but by this point we all knew he was soft in the center.

"These are real. There's no point in throwing wooden grenades any longer if you plan to graduate. We waited as long as we could. You need to know how to pull the pin, how long to count, and then what to do once you've got a live grenade in your hands. I'll take you five at a time, at first." He paused. "Anyone got any experience with the M1914?"

Masha smiled at me, but neither of us said anything.

"Well then, you five in front, come up here." That was Masha, Alsu, Muravyeva, a woman named Pul'khova whom I had barely spoken with, and me. He picked up a container of grenades—a six-pack—and carried it away from the others.

We followed him to an embankment made of sandbags and logs. It was dug into the sand chest-deep, and we went in, suddenly closed off from the world. I could barely hear the waves of the sea down here, and the sky was only a narrow strip of blue.

A trench.

Sergeant Zapilov popped open the container to reveal the six grenades nestled inside like eggs.

My heart beat with the characteristics. Weight: 580 grams. Length: 235 milimeters. Filling: 320 grams of TNT. Timing delay: 3.5–4 seconds. Effective range: 15 meters. It was like a poem I'd had to memorize in school, but one with a deadly cadence. 235mm was about the length of my forearm, and 580 grams was about the weight of a half-empty bottle of wine. Amazing that something so small could be so destructive.

The sergeant pulled a rolled-up sheet of paper out of the container and passed it around. I laughed when it reached me, and when his mouth quirked in response, I said, "Gubina probably packed this box."

He looked to Masha, who tapped the bottom of the paper over a smudged bit of ink. "Did you?"

Her cheek dimpled. "It has a line from a Pushkin poem at the bottom, so yes."

"You two worked at the factory?" he asked. When we nodded, he took the paper and handed it to the other three recruits. "And you added poetry to the sheets?"

"Something else for the soldiers to read. Those that could."

The sergeant shook his head, but he was smiling. "What did *you* do, Pavlova?"

"I poured the TNT." I waggled my fingers at him because they still bore a faint trace of gold.

"No wonder you can throw it like a mother—" he paused, and his teeth flashed between cracked lips. "Ever thrown a live one?"

I shook my head. He pulled a grenade out, and the other women stepped back. We'd been shooting for weeks, hitting each other with our fists and crawling beneath barbed wire, but the moment a real grenade was handed over, everyone got scared.

I took the grenade. The pin was still in.

"You know what to do?" he asked.

"In theory." I held it close and looked up out of the trench. "Who are we supposed to throw it at?"

"You murderous girl," he said, still grinning. He pointed at a small hillock of sand, halfway between the trench and the water's edge. No one was around for at least fifty meters, so if my throw went wide, no one would be harmed. Not that my throws ever went wide. "Know how long you've got? And the effective range?"

Muravyeva spoke up. "Three and a half seconds, about. And . . . fifteen meters. If you're twenty meters away, you'll be unharmed."

The sergeant snorted. "I wouldn't say you'd be 'unharmed,' exactly, but you might not be dead."

I lifted the grenade. It was time. "Take cover." The others moved backward to a spot where the trench curved sharply. Masha stayed.

"Get back," I told Masha. When she shook her head, I saw the confident girl from the factory courtyard, holding court with her paper girls.

"I want to watch."

Behind her, Muravyeva peeked from around the corner, her dark eyes assessing everything.

If anything happened to Masha, it would be my fault. If she didn't listen to me now, how would she react during battle? Not to mention the rest of my platoon—I had to consider how I looked to them, whether they'd see me as weak or indecisive.

"Gubina," I snapped. "Take cover."

Her eyes widened with hurt for a fraction of a second before she gave me a nod and joined the others behind the corner of the trench.

Holding the grenade tight against my chest, I pulled the pin. As long as I didn't let go of the lever, it'd stay inert, but once the lever lifted, it would start the firing mechanism, which set off an unstoppable chain reaction that funneled its way down to the charge at the base of the grenade. I knew all this, but the reality of it in my bare hands made my heart race.

I stood up straight, took aim, and lobbed the grenade at the sandy hill. One. The sergeant yanked me down into the trench. Two. I held my breath. Three. Any moment now. Four—*boom!* The grenade exploded, sending a cloud of sand ten meters high. When I popped up to see the result, I couldn't suppress a triumphant whoop. I pulled myself out of the trench and ran over to the newly formed pit in the ground.

Bits of scrap metal lay scattered across the sand and half of the hillock was dented. Tiny craters lay all around the area where the shrapnel had fallen. If there'd been anyone there, they would've been minced.

The others stayed in the trench, but Sergeant Zapilov came up behind me. "It's one thing to make one, and another to make one go boom, right?"

"Yes." I might have made that exact grenade. Maybe it was still winter then, and my fingers were frozen and caked with explosive, and I'd thought it would save a Russian life. Or it might have been a rainy day, and this was one of the grenades I'd filled quickly, thinking only of my quota, or thinking of the revolution. It didn't matter now. My heart was racing, my mind running and stumbling over the months I'd spent making grenades. None of it compared to this.

"You got that down, I think. Let's teach the others."

We each got one throw with a live grenade before the sergeant took another group. Everyone did well, although Alsu was visibly more nervous than the rest. When we moved to the next station, she whispered, "That was the scariest thing I've ever done. All I could think about was how I'd kill us all if I dropped it by accident."

"I was afraid of that too. I'm sure we all were. Fortunately, we won't be doing that all the time. Just when it's needed. You're fine with a rifle, and that's more important."

While I marched my platoon back to the barracks, I caught Masha's gaze. Her mouth curved up on one side, and she shrugged the tiniest bit, and I knew that although she hadn't liked doing what I said, she understood. At least for now.

JUNE 17, 1917

Dinner that night was boiled. All of it: the potatoes, the chicken, and the cabbage. I shoveled it into my mouth with one eye on Bochkareva, who ate with the officers on the other side of the dining hall, and one eye on my own soldiers.

"This is the best meal I've ever had," moaned Masha beside me.

"You say that every meal," said Korlova, on her other side.

"When you're starving, everything tastes good." This came from Pul'khova, who rarely spoke up. Most of those sitting around me had been truly hungry at one point recently, and they all nodded in agreement.

"Hey, Pavlova," asked Korlova, leaning forward so she

could see me around Masha. "What do you think about Avilo-va's platoon? They lost three more soldiers today."

"I guess they weren't really soldiers," I said after I swallowed.

"But why are they leaving now? It hasn't gotten any harder the past few days. Not really."

"The ones who are leaving are from Avilova's Women's Rights Committee," Masha said. "Maybe they've decided this isn't the best way to convince men we should have the same rights as them."

I laughed. "It's not the easiest way, for sure."

"They're fools," Masha said quietly.

"You don't agree with them?" asked Pul'khova.

"No, I do," she answered, "but I don't like how they're using the battalion to get what they want. Proving we can fight won't do the rest of the country's women any good. Also, I doubt any of them come from poor families. They aren't fighting for *all* women's rights, but for *their* rights."

I thought of how Sergeant Bochkareva couldn't read, and how Muravyeva, thorn of my side, had traded her only civilian dress for a stack of postcards so she could write to her mother, whom she'd left behind. Muravyeva was farther down the table, but she was close enough to hear us. She looked to be focusing on her plate, but I could tell by the way she slowed her fork that she'd understood Masha's point.

"Do you think they are fighting for Tatar women?" asked Alsu, although judging by the way she eyed Avilova, she knew the answer to that.

"They're fighting for Russia like we are," I said. "If they want to fight for more, that's fine with me."

"But why are some of them leaving?" asked Korlova again. "That's what I don't understand."

Then Muravyeva looked up at us. "It's because of General Order Number One. The army is supposed to let the recruits form committees to make decisions now, but Bochkareva said she won't allow it. Avilova and Bochkareva were arguing about it yesterday." She shrugged. "Seemed like Avilova lost."

"Well, a little humility might do her good," said Masha. "She's always looking down her nose at me. Ever since I told her not to include me in her group."

"She's a little snotty," I admitted, "but I think it's because she feels like she has to be strong for her women." As I said this, I looked at the table behind ours, where Avilova ate with her platoon. She still had over forty soldiers, and they looked at her like she was a grand duchess. "I mean, *she* hasn't quit, so she must have accepted whatever Bochkareva said about Order Number One."

"I think," added Alsu, "it can be difficult for women who already have some power to understand those who've never had it. And then to give it up . . . is not easy. But I think for our Avilova, it is something she can do."

"I still don't know why they quit," mumbled Korlova. "The food's good."

After an evening of rifle drills in the courtyard, we were finally released to our barracks. It had been one of those days that'd flown by but also felt like it had been a century since breakfast. As we were heading inside, I yanked off my cap and tucked it under an arm, grateful for the chance to scratch at my itchy scalp.

Masha reached up to brush her hair off her shoulder like she used to and found nothing there. She laughed. "I feel like I've given up a magical power I once had."

"Nonsense," snapped Alsu. She took the both of us by our arms and brought us to the door. "You've only traded it temporarily for a gun." She swung her bright gray eyes on me. "Did you see those targets Masha destroyed earlier?"

Masha had a natural talent with her rifle. She was so good, in fact, I was worried Bochkareva would have her transferred to a sniper platoon. "How did this happen, you being such a good shot?"

"You're just jealous," she said. We'd reached our benches and were setting the rifles onto the gun rack. She took mine and set it beside hers, then Alsu's.

"Well, it's surprising! You never fired a gun in your life before we came here."

"Yes I have."

"When?"

"At my uncle's dacha. He taught me to shoot ducks. What I want to know, however, is how Katya got good at throwing things. Grenades, in particular. She doesn't have a family dacha—"

"Yes, I do." A memory came to me then, of the wooden cabin, of soft, filtered sunlight warming up the kitchen, of mint and dill growing wild amongst the strawberries. Of my mother singing as she snipped roses off the trellis to put on the table. "I just haven't been there in a long, long time."

I couldn't look up at them as I spoke. I hadn't been to the dacha since my mother left, since my father stopped tucking me in to bed, since we'd stopped being a family that went to the countryside together in the summer.

Liddikova's platoon walked past us then, laughing, and we were forced onto our benches to give them room to pass. The dark memory, the moment of my mother running out the front door and into a carriage with the man in the blue scarf—it was gone.

I peeled my boots and trousers off like a scab.

"Olga told Prince Mal that she was feeling merciful, and would not require such an expensive tribute after all. Instead, as a token of goodwill between their people—"

"She had to be beautiful if they still believed this woman."

"As I said, she was very intelligent."

"What sort of token did she ask for?"

"Birds."

13

JUNE 18, 1917

WE marched as four separate platoons with our men's boots slapping into the pavement and our fists swishing against our hips. Each of us carried her rifle nestled against an aching shoulder, some marked beneath her blouse with plum-colored bruises. My soldiers kept in line, watching the person to her side out of the corner of her eye and stomping just a little louder on her left foot. After an hour of this, we reached the shore and the pine-scented obstacle course.

While Sergeant Bochkareva split us apart and went to report to the officer there for our review, I watched how my platoon readied itself. Muravyeva stood in the thick of them all, making sure pants' hems were securely tucked into boots or puttees. Alsu spoke with one of the girls who had sprained her ankle a few days ago. Masha—Gubina—was squatting down and stretching her legs, a position she would never have tried in skirts. Every few moments, each of them glanced my way and made eye contact. They carefully stacked their rifles into one another, making cones, and then made their way to the starting line.

We were ready.

Bochkareva belted out the instructions. "Get through it as fast as you can, and don't leave anyone behind! Platoon leaders, that means you! You have fifteen minutes!"

The officers from headquarters stood off to the side, arms crossed and eyebrows ticked. One of them swung a stopwatch from a chain and lifted a whistle to his lips.

With a rush of boots and flying sand, we ran together to the first obstacle: the wall. It didn't matter if any of us were tired. I decided to go ahead of my platoon so that I could help them across, so I clenched my fists around one of the three ropes and pulled, grunting like an old man. My boots scrabbled at the wooden planks, but there weren't any footholds, so I pulled, harder. My elbow popped, unleashing a torrent of pain, but in the back of my mind I heard Ilya yelling at me when I was fourteen years old, "Pain is only a weakness!"

I would not allow myself to be weak. I couldn't.

Gritting my teeth, I put everything I had into my arms and tugged myself up until I could take hold of the top plank. It dug into my palms, but the pain was nothing. It was weakness. I pulled myself higher, my knees pushed into the narrow ledge, and then I was there. I was breathless, but I was three meters feet off the ground, straddling a narrow plank of pine. Next came the women of my platoon. As each one climbed up and over, I patted her shoulder and urged her on. Then it was Alsu's turn. With each foot she climbed, her lips got paler and thinner.

"Almost there," I said.

"I don't," she gasped, "know why. We have. To climb. So high." I yanked her by the shoulders, helped her over the plank, and slapped the rope over the other side so she could climb down.

"Hard part's over!" I yelled after her.

"*Five minutes!*" a man shouted.

When Muravyeva climbed over, she took the rope farthest from me. Looking directly at her hands, she clambered up like a squirrel, cocked an eyebrow at me, and dropped to the other side.

"Beat you there!" she called at me over her shoulder. Coming from Muravyeva, this was downright friendly.

When the last from my platoon made it over, I dropped down the other side and ran. All around us the trainers shouted, taunting us, encouraging us, screaming out the ticking seconds. Over them all came Bochkareva's voice, weaving through the sand-thick air like a hawk after a knot of sparrows.

The next obstacle was low to the ground. Real barbed wire crossed over a trail at knee height, and my platoon was already in the thick of it. There was a bit of a line as they waited for the person ahead to get through, so I ran up alongside the wire, yelling at them to keep their faces down, to move, to dig in with their knees. Then it was my turn, and I dropped to the ground and began sawing myself forward on elbows and knees, my stomach dragging in the sand. My cap got caught for a second, and when I reached up to tug it free, I was finally happy my hair was gone. My teeth were coated in sand and my knees were on fire, but my scalp was safe.

"What're you smiling at, Pavlova?" Sergeant Zapilov shouted. I ignored him and kept going.

"*Ten minutes!*"

When I was out from beneath the barbed wire, I didn't bother brushing the sand off. I ran between the dunes, leaping along the wooden posts set up in the smooth tide of the sea, nearly slipping into the cold water, and then raced to another climbing obstacle. Alsu was stuck again, but just barely. I reached up beneath her and shoved, and she toppled to the other side. Once I was over, I helped her up. She eyed me grimly until I dragged her after me.

"One more," I panted, and she nodded wordlessly.

Masha was ahead of us punching and kicking the straw-stuffed dummies with the German Iron Cross painted on the front. She would hit one till it swayed on its reed pole, and then run to another, zig-zagging across that part of the field. While Alsu ran in to join her, I scanned the area for my platoon. Most had gone through the finish line already, but a few were still at the dummies. When I checked at the last climbing structure, I saw Muravyeva clutching her thigh with one hand and hoisting herself over the with the other. She wasn't moving fast enough, and our time was running out.

I climbed up the structure.

"What's wrong?"

Wet sand streaked across her cheekbones. "Cramp," she said, avoiding my eyes. "Just a cramp."

"*Thirteen!*"

I reached down and offered her my hand.

"I can do it," she said.

"Take it." When she continued to inch her way up, I thrust out my hand again. "Muravyeva, take my hand!"

She finally let go with one hand and clamped onto my wrist. I yanked her up. My arm was straining, and my legs were latched onto the wooden planks so hard I was afraid they'd break, but I got her to the top. She paused for a second, sucked in a deep breath, and then nodded in gratitude.

"Let's move!" I said.

"*Fourteen!*"

Together we rammed into the dummies, and when we crossed the finish line, she was a half-step ahead. I was the last in my platoon, as planned. It took everything I had to move my legs, to breathe, but then someone was clasping my hand and pulling me away from the line.

Sergeant Bochkareva was the only clean woman in sight. She had dirt on her boots, sure, but she didn't have sand caked into her short hair. My uniform was soaked with sweat and my fingernails were split and filled with grime. My arms felt like they were going to fall off.

I had never, ever, felt so alive.

Energy poured through us, and we stood around while the sergeant told us what we did right or wrong, eyeing each other in surprise. We'd made it through. Hundreds of women made it through the army's obstacle course. If we could do that on just a few hours' sleep, we could do so much more.

That energy spread to the instructors, too. Their eyes shone brighter, and Sergeant Bochkareva couldn't shake off her grin. She had her battalion.

We'd made it over the wall, across the deep, soft sand, and under the wire. We hadn't won the war yet, but we'd won our first battle.

"Soldiers!" Bochkareva shouted again, and my mind shot back to her. "Tomorrow, you're doing it again." I grinned at Masha. Let them order us to do this every day. "With rifles."

The groan was loud enough they could probably hear us back in Petrograd. I studied the obstacle course again, wondering how I could do half the things with an extra ten pounds on my back. At the moment, I was too tired to carry a silk chemise.

Sergeant Bochkareva put her hand up for silence. The corner of her mouth twitched like she was trying not to laugh.

"You'll do it with rifles, and you'll be faster than you were today. I have faith." She turned on her heels and marched to where the lieutenants were smoking cigarettes. "Especially now." She said the last words under her breath, but I was close enough to hear it.

Back at the barracks, we took turns at the bathhouse. Even with only a quarter of an inch of hair, it was hard to get the sand the out of my scalp. I dunked my whole head in a bucket of luke-warm water and rubbed furiously. It felt like heaven. I came up to breathe, then dunked my head back in again, wishing I could save up moments like this for later.

"I will trade you everything on my lunch plate if you mas-sage my feet for me right now." Masha leaned against the wall, fully dressed but for her bare feet.

"Massage your own feet." I laughed and rubbed the towel over my head.

With an overly dramatic sigh, she rubbed her feet for a few seconds before wrapping on fresh portyanki. "When this is all over, I am going to stay in bed for three days and do nothing but read books and eat cake."

Alsu sat down beside her. "I'm taking my three daughters to Greece."

Masha and I turned to look at her in surprise.

"Why Greece?" I asked.

"It's always warm there, and no one has to really work. They go fishing all day, kicking their feet in the warm ocean." She stared me down. "And don't tell me otherwise. I want to believe this is the truth about Greece."

"Sounds heavenly to me," said Masha. "I'll have to visit you there."

147

As I buttoned up my collar, I turned away from them, hoping they'd move on to another topic. I'd always wanted to study chemistry in Paris, like Marie Curie, but the war had shattered my plans. When my babushka died and I left the university to take work at the factory, my professor said the time out of school would rot my brain, that I would forget everything he'd taught me. He even threatened that the TNT would poison my blood, killing me slowly.

Maybe there wasn't anything on the other side of this war. Not for me.

"Katya?" Alsu asked. "What about you?"

I made myself smile before I turned back around. "Oh, I'm planning on an entire career in the army. Officer bars. Maybe a horse." They both looked stunned, even Masha.

"You want to do this for the rest of your life?" Masha asked.

I tucked my shirt in. "Or maybe I'll just come back here, live off my father's money, and take warm baths and drink buckets of honey tea."

"You'll end up back in school," Masha said, tying her boot laces. "I bet my life on it. You're destined to be a great chemist."

Instead of responding, I held up my rifle. "How are we going to keep these things clean tomorrow?"

Alsu peered down her barrel and frowned. "I don't know how we'll keep the mud out of this."

Avilova made her way between the benches. She caught my eye and waved a small stack of letters at me.

"These came for you," she said. "One is a telegram from the front."

My hand shook when I took the letters. I sat back down on my makeshift bed with Masha and Alsu flanking me.

"Is that from your father?" Masha asked, pointing at the smaller one. I nodded and ran a finger over my name on the envelope. "He must have found out, then."

It didn't matter if they read it too, I decided, and ripped it open.

```
Keep your head down. You are not St. Olga.

                                    —V. Pavlov
```

No, because this isn't a revenge story! I wanted to yell to him, sending my voice across the fields and forests.

"He must be proud of you," Alsu said, gently squeezing one of my hands in hers. "If he didn't believe you could do this, wouldn't he have told you to leave? Or found some way for the army to take you out? All he had to do was say you were under-age and didn't have his permission."

"If he did that, he'd have everyone saying both of his children were cowards."

Alsu got up and went to her bed, where she began rifling through her little bag of private belongings. She pulled out a prayer book and opened it to where a small photograph had been stuck in as a bookmark. She handed me the prayer book, pointing at the photograph. It was of a man in a Tatar uniform, with a large woolen hat covering half of his head. His eyes were calm and focused away from the camera.

"That's Karim. He was looking at me when we had this photo made." I was afraid to ask the obvious question, but she answered it anyway. "He died in October, in the Crimea." Her voice was softer and it was suddenly my turn to comfort her.

"I'm sure he was brave and loved you very much."

Nodding, she blinked away the wetness in her eyes. "If he were here now, he would not be telling me to stay home with our daughters. He'd understand that I cannot just sit and wait for the war to end—he'd let me go. Like your papa."

Masha, never one to be left out of a conversation, took the prayer book from me and studied Karim's photograph. "Is this why you want to go to Greece?"

Alsu sighed. "It's a nice dream, isn't it? To see my girls wading in warm waters. To see them happy again. For that, I'll do anything."

"Who are they with now?" I asked, feeling for the girls.

"With my family. They have many cousins to play with." Then she took the prayer book, gently ran a finger over Karim's face, and put it back in her little cotton bag. "Do you have something to keep that in?" she asked, gesturing at the telegram. The telegram had become a triangle, just like the last one Papa had sent me. I flicked it between my fingers, over and under, and then slid it into my leather munitions bag.

My father had, in very few words, given me permission to fight.

Not that I needed it.

"Who sent you the other one?" Masha asked. "It's local."

I knew, even though there wasn't a sender's name on the outside. "Sergei," I said, and I curled away from her so I could open it without an audience. I could almost feel her eyes rolling at my backside.

> Katya, please be careful. I don't
> want you to get hurt.
>
> —S. Grigorev

Did he mean at the front? Or were the Bolsheviks planning something to keep us away from the train?

"Did he send his love?" Masha asked with a yawn.

"In a way."

I couldn't tell her. We shared so many things, but the extent of my involvement with the Bolsheviks wasn't one of them, so I let her believe Sergei's letter was full of poetry and slipped it under my pillow.

JUNE 21, 1917

We were done. Training was over, and today we would march to Saint Vasily's Cathedral and receive our blessing.

"Where's my belt buckle?" Masha brushed by, quickly, and dug through her bag once more. "I can't find it anywhere." The barracks buzzed with activity, with soldiers polishing boots and pinning the new emblems onto caps. In the corner, Dubrovskaya bent her dark head and finished sewing the last of the letters onto our battalion's silk banner.

I leaned against the wall with my feet pulled close and wrapped on my portyanki until every toe and both ankles were well covered. "Did you ask Alsu?"

"She hasn't seen it either."

"Did you check inside your boots?"

"What?" She paused and shook her left boot. It rattled. "How did you know?"

Shrugging, I slipped my feet into my boots and stood up. "Just a guess."

She whirled around, picked her belt up off her bed, and put

it on around her tunic. "We only have two minutes before we have to be outside."

I rubbed at the top of my head. "It's a good thing we don't have to worry about doing our hair then." She had two minutes, but I only had one. As platoon leader, I had to be out there before my soldiers. I slapped my cap on, straightened my lapels, tugged my tunic down over my hips, and went to the rifle rack to get my rifle. I was out in under thirty seconds and my nerves didn't catch up to me until I reached the courtyard.

My heart was beating too quickly. It was just a parade. Just a long walk to the center of Petrograd. Just a peek inside the cathedral. But I could hear the horses clomping down the road outside our little training haven, and I knew it was more than just a walk, just a parade. The Saint Georgi's Cavaliers were going to lead us, and we would also be accompanied by the Ninth Reserve Cavalry, two Cossack regiments, a few other regiments and even some cadets. But the main attraction today would be the newly trained, shiny and perfect Battalion of Death of Maria Bochkareva.

My soldiers milled in front of me, waiting for me give them the word.

"Fall in!" My voice shook, but I didn't think they noticed. Their complexions were either paler or ruddier than normal, but everyone shone with fresh polish. Masha, at the front in the third column, looked over my shoulder, careful to keep her eyes on the horizon. She'd learned well.

I turned around and waited while the other three platoons got in line. Avilova's platoon looked much the same as mine, and I gave her a nod to show her I was ready. Then Bochkareva came forward.

"They're waiting in the street for us! Thousands of proud

Russians waiting to cheer for you!" She shouted so that everyone could hear. "Look sharp! Stay in step! And do exactly what your platoon leaders tell you to do!" Then, even louder, "Forward, March!"

The order came down to Avilova and me, and we in turn had our platoons marching forward, one after the other, out the gates.

There were no cars, wagons, or trams in our way, but there were more horses than I could count. The cavalrymen looked smart in their dress uniforms with the red stripe down the side of the leg, their shiny boots and swords, their rifles slung over their backs. Their massive, snorting warhorses had been brushed till they shone. Their size did nothing to still my nerves. Once they passed, we filed in behind them, making a Column Right directly onto the street.

Other regiments marched behind us, noticeable only by the sound of their leaders' calls, deeper than any woman's, but I didn't turn to look. I had to keep my women in step and in line so that when we were seen, we looked good. We had to look good, because everything was riding on our shoulders. Not only did we have to pass muster as basic soldiers, we had to meet the higher standard of a death battalion—a *suicide battalion*. We had to prove to everyone that we weren't weak, we weren't hysterical, and we weren't afraid. We were disciplined, fit, and deadly.

We marched at a good pace. The closer we got to Saint Isaac's Square, the more people there were standing on the sides of the streets, waving flags and cheering for us.

"Those are real Russian girls!" someone shouted.

"Show the men what courage means!"

When the road opened up into Saint Isaac's Square, and the domed golden cathedral loomed over us all, it took all my self-control to keep my face neutral. There were thousands of people. The collective roar of their voices gave me goosebumps, and I couldn't hold back a small smile. If it weren't for the cavalry leading the way, I'm not sure they would have made enough room for us to march through. Fortunately, people backed up when a warhorse was approaching.

The cavalry stopped in front of the cathedral's door, and for a split second, I wondered if they would ride the horses straight inside. Bochkareva called us to a halt, someone pulled open the cathedral doors, and we filed in.

I'd never gone in the cathedral with a weapon before, and the rifle felt heavier, the stock slippery. I gripped it tight, thumbing the stock. The malachite and lapis lazuli columns shone, framing the iconostasis that decorated the altar. Without intending to, I searched out the icon my grandmother had ticked off on her list. It was still there. She was not, but I tucked away that pang knowing she might have been the only babushka in the city to approve of a battalion of women carrying rifles into the nave.

Avilova, Liddikova, Mussorgskaya, and I joined Bochkareva and the two company commanders at the front. We were greeted by the Archbishop Veniamin of Petrograd, the highest-ranking priest in the city.

It all happened like a waking dream. Bochkareva was promoted to the rank of sub-lieutenant and given a revolver and a saber. Dubrovskaya came forward and presented the red-and-black banner with Saint Georgi on one side and our skull-and-crossbones emblem on the other. The words "Women's Battalion of Death of Maria Bochkareva" were embroidered around the skull, and it stuck to Dubrovskaya's legs while the Archbishop waved his hand over the golden fringe.

Then it was over and we filed outside into the square. The army orchestra started up with the "La Marseillaise"—a song of the revolution, of fighting tyranny and foreign invasion. Each beat of the drums echoed in my stomach, filling me with a sense of unity. I was not alone anymore. I had a band of sisters now, and together we would go to fight.

We turned off Nevsky Prospekt and were marching toward the Field of Mars when the parade came to a stop. My platoon marched in place for a moment before I halted them so that I could take a look up ahead. We nearly filled the street, so to get a clear view, I had to get close to the sidewalk and the throngs of people who'd lined up to watch us.

A car blocked the road ahead, but no one sat inside it. Red flags flapped from poles stuck into the seats, and around the car, like a hive of hornets, swarmed a group of men with red armbands. They were shouting.

"End to the war!"

"No Kerensky Offensive!"

Bolsheviks. This wasn't just a blockade. In an instant, I knew this was what Sergei's note had been warning me against.

"Sergeant Bochkareva!" I shouted in warning, but she'd already run to the front to yell at the men blocking our passage. Turning around, I called Masha out of the platoon and put her in charge, then joined Bochkareva. She and Lieutenant Ornilov were in a shouting match with a pair of factory workers. The men's cheeks were ruddy with either drink or excitement.

I scanned the crowd near the car for Sergei and was glad not to find him.

"You have no authority to be in our way!" screamed Bochkareva. Lieutenant Ornilov stood slightly behind her. Despite the fact she was junior in rank to Lieutenant Ornilov, she was clearly the person in command.

"Disband your battalion, woman!" the worker said.

"Get out of our way, or I will shoot!" she shouted back. She took a step closer, showing no fear. This was going to end badly.

When I came up beside Lieutenant Ornilov, she glanced over her shoulder at me. "Tell your soldiers to go to arms."

The command was like a blow to the gut. We'd trained to fight Germans, not our own people.

"Hey girl," the man snarled, "tell your commander here there's no more need for a war. Tell her how the Bolsheviks will save Russia." He spoke to me, but his eyes were on Bochkareva.

She stood her ground, her nostrils flaring. "To arms, Pavlova." Her eyes bored into mine.

I saluted and rejoined my platoon, each step pulling at me as though a string had been tied between me and Bochkareva. It was growing tighter and tighter.

"Katya!" a man's voice called from the side. "Katya, you have to get them away!"

There were too many people lined up along the sidewalk, but I searched among the faces as casually as I could, still heading toward my platoon.

There. Between an old woman and a cadet. Sergei, shouting at me.

He leaned as far forward as he could, but the cadet was holding him back. "You've got to—"

Bang! A gunshot cracked down the street, the sound echoing from building to building. Someone had shot into our ranks, but no one fell. The Bolsheviks began shouting at one another while the shocked spectators scattered like ice cracking on a pond. I whirled on my platoon to keep them in line.

A few flinched, their eyes flicking to mine, but they did not break formation.

"Ready!" I called. Fifty-five women lowered their rifles and pulled the bolts back and forth. "Aim!" Chins jammed into stocks, eyes narrowed, fingers resting near the trigger.

I looked to Bochkareva, but she did not call the order to shoot. She held her arm at her side, grimacing as she watched something over my shoulder.

The street began to rumble. Behind us raced the Cossacks, splitting their ranks of horses to flow around us. I stepped into my platoon to avoid the pounding hooves and watched as the cavalry raced past us, their red stripes flashing and their sharp sabers angled forward.

The Bolsheviks jumped into their car and sped away in a flurry of dust, pursued by the mounted Cossacks.

"Rifles down!" I shouted. With a collective sigh, my entire battalion disarmed.

Bochkareva's arm was bleeding. Lieutenant Ornilov offered her his handkerchief and she shook her head, then spit in the street.

"I'll get it seen to," she muttered. Then she shouted for us all to hear, "Forward, March!"

I tried to look for where I'd seen Sergei, but he was gone.

Back in the barracks, I pulled off my belt and dropped it beside my cap, wishing for the twentieth time or so that I could take a hot bath, eat a large lunch, and take a nap in my own bed at home.

"That was exhausting," I said.

"I can't believe no one was hurt," Alsu said.

"Except for Bochkareva, Shostakova, and Lieutenant Ornilov," Masha added.

Alsu shrugged that off. "They weren't hurt badly."

"We were shot at by our own people," I said darkly.

"Those aren't our people," Masha said. She nearly ripped off her shirt trying to get the buttons undone. "Those were Bolsheviks."

"Bolsheviks *are* our people, Masha," I said. "They believe in all of us, not just the wealthy, not just the lucky. They want us out of the war so we can focus on ourselves. So we can fix Russia."

"When did you turn into a socialist?" she snapped.

"I'm not," I said, looking everywhere but at her.

"But you're defending the Bolsheviks. The people who were just shooting at us."

"I don't know what to believe sometimes, Masha!"

My stomach ached, and I wanted to run outside, but there was nowhere I could go. And I would never run from my battalion.

"That's the way of the world," Alsu said. She smiled at me, both understanding my confusion and urging that I let it go.

As if in concession, Masha pulled off her cap and rubbed at her short hair till it stood back up again. "Well, you looked out for us back there, and I suppose that's what matters right now."

I nodded slowly. I didn't know whether the Bolsheviks were right about the future. It was hard for me to separate a lifetime of absorbing my father's point of view from what I'd more recently learned during the Women's March and the abdication of the Tsar. But for now, in this moment, I was a soldier. I was going to the war. That much I knew for certain.

Masha lay down flat on her bench. "I will never forget this day."

"Do you remember when your father's unit marched by?" I asked.

"Yes," she said, smiling. "It was beautiful the way they all marched so straight, so sharp. But today, we were those soldiers. We were the ones marching across the square."

"We were sharper. Better. I remember his unit. They were good, but they weren't as good as we are. That's what I was trying to say. I've seen so many military parades—more than anyone ever should—and I have to say, this was the best one. I wish . . ." I couldn't finish it. I swallowed and sat up to start pulling off my boots. My feet were too hot. I need a pot of cold water to soothe them, but that wasn't going to happen.

"You wish your father could have been there to see it." Masha knew exactly what I'd been about to say.

I bit my tongue. I would not be weak right now. I would not.

"He'll hear of it. There were photographers, and it'll be in the newspaper. And you're a platoon leader, so you'll stand out. Katya, he'll see you. He will! And he'll be proud."

I made a dismissive noise. She was wrong there, I was sure of it. He would find something lacking in me. I wouldn't be in step with my platoon, or my cap wouldn't be set at the right angle on my head, or I wouldn't have the proper bearing of a soldier. He'd grown bitter over the years, and always lashed out at perceived imperfection.

I wasn't perfect, but I would never desert.

"We'll soon find out what he thinks," I said, leaning back as I pulled off my boots. "We've been assigned to the Tenth Army at the front. That's where he is."

"Birds? But that's silly. They'd just fly away."

"Olga said, 'Give me three pigeons and three sparrows from each house.' Prince Mal was eager to make such a gift, as he'd become poor in his quest to win Olga as his bride."

"And his people had that many pigeons and sparrows? Each house?"

"So it is said in the Holy Chronicles. And they gave them to her."

"Then what did she do? Cut off the birds' heads and throw them at Prince Mal?"

"There once was a peaceful monk named Kirill . . ."

"Papa!"

14

JUNE 22, 1917

THE last day in Petrograd was a strange combination of hurry and wait. We acquired two machine guns with gunners, tents, and other supplies, which were carted to the railway station. We marched from our barracks to the train station, and on the way were harassed again by Bolshevik bystanders, but this time no one blocked our path or attacked us.

As we arrived, I couldn't help thinking how much had changed since I came here with Maxim. I no longer worked in a factory, and he was no longer in the army. I was proudly on my way to the front, and he had slipped out the back door. I was on my way to our father, and Maxim had deserted. I'd been left behind by everyone in my family. But now, I had comrades.

My platoon filled an entire train car, but I was missing one of my soldiers. I had seen her that morning, but now that I thought about it, I hadn't seen her when we formed up in the courtyard before we left the barracks. I got a queasy feeling in my stomach as I underlined her name on my clipboard.

"Pavlova." I turned and found Bochkareva in full gear, her

new pistol on her belt and her officer's insignia gleaming on her cap. "You're missing Kosik."

"Yes," I said, curious how she knew.

"She slipped out after breakfast. Her mother came, crying about something to do with her little sister, and she left with her."

We hadn't even left Petrograd yet, and we'd already lost a soldier. "She didn't tell me she was leaving."

"She told me. If she can't bear to leave Petrograd, I can't have her in the battalion. Volunteers only. Now get on board." Then she turned and went to her train car.

I struck Kosik's name off my list. I would miss her, but maybe it was for the best. She was too sweet, too bubbly for this, and if we were going to see a battle like what I was expecting, it could destroy her.

I had one hand on the train car handle and one hoisting my gear up onto the steps when I heard my name being called from the platform.

"Katya! Katya, wait!" I released the handle like it was on fire. The voice belonged to Sergei.

I nudged my gear onto the train and then stepped back down onto the platform. The engineers were still walking up and down the cars, checking to make sure everything was in order. We had a minute.

Sergei was in the same clothes he'd been wearing when I saw him last, but his student cap was gone. His hair flapped freely as he ran in long leaping strides toward me. "Wait!"

"Sergei." I forced my voice to remain calm.

"I had to see you before you left."

"Were you with your comrades out there, trying to keep us from getting on the train?"

He shook his head vehemently. "I've been here, trying to

162

find you. Do you know how many women there are getting on this train? And you all look the same!" He paused to look me over. "It suits you. The uniform. The rifle. If I didn't think this was a huge mistake, I'd applaud you."

I opened my mouth, then shut it. I pressed my back against the train handle, where it dug into my rolled-up overcoat.

He lifted my hands to his mouth and kissed the backs of my fingers. It was surprising, but after a month of soldier training, the gesture was more comforting than not. "I'm sorry," he continued. "I didn't know they were going to block your parade, or I would have been more specific. I knew they were planning something, but no one tells me details. I was watching you receive your battle flag when I heard Oleg talking about the others blocking your route. No one told them to do that. It wasn't right. It's—I don't know what to do anymore."

"Can't you report them to the Bolshevik leaders, then?"

"Oh, they know about it. I heard Lenin was furious, although he can't say anything in *Pravda* about it."

"Why not?"

He looked bewildered. "Because it would look as if he'd lost control over the Bolsheviks."

"Hasn't he, though?"

"The revolution is made up of people, and people don't work together like bees. Sometimes, there are rogues." He sighed. "I didn't want to part on a bad note. I know you're doing what you believe in, and you never criticized me for what *I* believed in."

I laughed. "Well, that's a lie."

"Maybe." His eyes danced. "When you get back, I'll put you right back to work, and we can continue arguing. Will you write to me?"

"I don't even know where to send it."

"Send it to the *Pravda* office."

An engineer called down the platform. "I have to go. Good-bye, Sergei." I climbed up the stairs and an attendant shut the door, but at the last second I leaned out its open glass window. "I'll look for you when I come back."

The whistle blew, so I missed whatever he said next, but he waved. I watched him grow smaller and smaller until he was gone, until the station was gone, and then, at last, Petrograd was gone.

In the train car, my soldiers whooped at me. I waved a hand dismissively, hoping to make light of the scene they'd been watching through their windows.

Sergei was only a friend, a comrade. I wasn't sure I wanted to write to him. Everything we'd shared before had been words on the wind. Letters had words you could touch and tuck beneath your pillow, if you had one.

Writing to him would mean opening a door that would be hard to shut. It would mean he meant more to me than I wanted to allow.

"You didn't tell me this Sergei fellow was so devoted," Masha said, suddenly at my side. She pulled me down onto a seat.

"You saved me a spot," I said, smiling brightly.

"You're the platoon commander. Of course you get a seat. Now don't change the subject."

"Sergei's not a subject. There's nothing to say about him."

I let Alsu take my kit and put it in the rack above, and I leaned back. So many days of preparation, and now we had a chance to rest. Possibly the last chance we would get. With a sigh, I shut my eyes.

"Have you been keeping company with him?" she asked. When I shook my head, she whacked me on the shoulder. "Katya! No one else had a young man running after them just as the train was about to leave."

"That's because their families were already here. They said their goodbyes. He just couldn't find me till the last moment." I didn't want to talk about Sergei or families, especially after what Masha had said the other day about the Bolsheviks. She was always so sure of herself, even if she switched sides from day to day.

Masha only snaked her hand around my upper arm and set her head on my shoulder. She smelled like lavender soap and gun oil, a bit of her old self and a bit of the new. I forced myself to stop thinking about Masha's certainty or of Sergei's lips on my fingers. I couldn't allow myself to have these soft feelings for him. This was the time to harden myself, to prepare for what I knew would take every gram of focus.

I leaned my head against the cold glass windowpane and watched the trees rush past in a blur of summer green. We were moving faster than I'd ever gone in my life. Not away, but *to*.

PART THREE
VALKYRIE

"I am not one of those who left their land
To the mercy of the enemy.
I was deaf to their gross flattery.
I won't grant them my songs."

—Anna Akhmatova, 1922

"Olga distributed the birds among her soldiers."

"I guess they were hungry."

"She told each man to tie a piece of sulfur bound with shreds of cloth to the foot of each bird."

"I knew she was going to do something strange."

"That night, Olga told her soldiers to light the bundles on fire and release the birds."

"Ooooh. And they—they all flew straight back home!"

"Each nest in each house caught on fire'."

"Olga was so wicked!"

"Yes."

"And also amazing."

15

JUNE 24, 1917
MOLODECHNO, BELARUS

IT took us two days on the train to reach the Tenth Army Headquarters. Each time we made a stop along the way, people greeted us with flowers and sweets, but as we got closer to our destination the warm greetings thinned and the insults from our fellow Russian soldiers increased.

The instant the train screeched to a stop in Molodechno, we were surrounded. Men waved rifles in the air, and others spat at the windows, making the dust run in sickening streaks down the glass. Bochkareva hopped off the train and started screaming at them.

"Go," I said to my soldiers. "Fall in behind her. She's clearing our way." We already had all our gear strapped on, ready to hop off, because by now we knew what to expect. Bochkareva clearly did too, because the curses she threw out were particularly creative and must have taken some time to string up onto her tongue.

I marched my women along the train car and we fell in behind Bochkareva. It didn't matter that we weren't in the correct order. We just needed to move. Avilova's platoon filled in behind mine, and we marched, hitching our greatcoats up and winching the straps on our rifles. One of the men shouted at me, "Hey whore, come shoot my rifle!"

I glared at him, noting he had no rifle.

He scowled, revealing a missing tooth. "Amazonian prude."

"How can I be both a whore *and* a prude?" I asked my platoon, trying to laugh as I said it. My soldiers were out of step and the formation was losing its cohesiveness. Before I could think of a way to bolster them, the man reached out at me and grabbed my sleeve. I spun and instinctively raised the stock of my rifle above his head. It would be so easy to smash it into him. "Talk to us *one more time*," I growled.

He backpedaled into the rest of the men, who laughed and shoved him to the ground.

"Capitalist slave!" he shouted, but by then we'd marched on by.

After a while, the insults and slurs blended into one giant voice that said, *Go home. Because you're here, we have to keep fighting and we are tired.* Of course, they didn't like that we were women, either, and they told us over and over what they'd like to do to us with their own, personal, guns.

They followed us until we reached the staff compound, a wooden building that looked more like a summer dacha than a military headquarters. A colonel came out and ordered the men to disperse. Then he shared some words with Bochkareva, who was as spitting mad as an alley cat.

Eventually, she told us to follow her and a private who'd been given orders to take us to our barracks. We walked through the encampment to two dilapidated buildings the army had left vacant for very obvious reasons.

"Holy Sister of War," said Masha when we walked inside. "This is worse than the barracks in Petrograd."

Two long benches lined the walls. Other than that, the building was empty. Not a chair, not a table, nothing. I gulped, and then let the women behind us come in. Their expressions said everything I was feeling.

"Pick a spot, head to toe," I said to them. "It's better than pitching tents. At least we'll be dry." Then I studied the rafters, just in case. There were a few suspicious spots, but it hadn't looked like rain outside. We might get lucky.

Once we'd unloaded our gear, Avilova sent a detail with Bochkareva to procure some food, as all we'd brought were bags of dry kasha and some tins of herring. On the way here I'd noticed that the fields were either picked clean or trampled, but I had hope there'd be something fresh.

They came back with a bag of sprouting potatoes and three handfuls of radishes, and after two days on a train it felt like a feast. By the time the sun lowered on the horizon, we had eaten enough to make it through the night. We sprawled in the grass and dirt, none of us wanting to go back into the empty barracks, despite the swarming flies outside. When night fell, we reluctantly returned to the rickety building. I laid out my greatcoat on the bench and tried not to roll off onto the floor. Masha slept at my feet.

"Ladies!" a man shouted from outside half an hour later. "Come on out!"

Bochkareva's low voice cut through the darkness. "Don't respond. Don't leave your beds."

"*Beds*," one of the women chuckled. I almost did too.

"Hey! Lady soldiers! We want to see you out of uniform!"

"Go shove a rifle up your ass!" responded Bochkareva, loud enough for those outside to hear.

Then the banging started. They pounded on the door so

hard it bowed inward. We slid along our benches to the farthest end of the room.

All of us but Bochkareva. She jumped up from her spot, pulled her pistol out of its holster, and threw open the door just as a volley of rocks smashed the front windows. Men started reaching in through the window, trying to grab at whatever part of a woman they could get.

"Leave my troops alone!" Bochkareva shouted. She cocked the pistol. "Pavlova, get your rifle."

Swallowing down my alarm, I pulled my rifle from its spot under the bench and ran to her side. She glanced at me and nodded.

"Load it and aim."

I rammed the magazine in, stepped into the doorway, and took aim at the nearest man. His tunic hung loose over his trousers, which were falling out of his boots. He smirked at me. I pulled the bolt back, felt the first bullet slide into position, and set the bolt back.

Click.

"Hey now." He raised his hands. "We're all on the same side."

"If any of them move any closer, shoot that one," Bochkareva said. "I have authority from Colonel Zakrezhevskii to protect my troops, and if it means shooting some bastards at midnight, then so be it."

Avilova appeared at my side with her rifle and aimed at another man. "I like shooting bastards," she said, a bit louder than necessary. "It's good practice."

The men moved backward, slipping into the shadows cast by our lantern. Out of the side of her mouth, Bochkareva told us to stay put, then went back inside.

"Are we staying here all night?" Avilova asked after a moment.

I would have shrugged if that wouldn't have altered my aim. "I doubt it. Even these men have to sleep."

A minute later, Bochkareva came back outside dressed in full uniform. She was tying on extra cartridges to her belt while holding the pistol with a few fingers. It rolled forward with the weight of the grip. "You two, stand guard for thirty minutes. After that, each of you will choose one soldier from your platoon to take your place, and so on till morning."

"Where are you going?" I asked her.

"To the Colonel."

She was gone before I had could tell her that might not be a good idea, although she wouldn't have listened to me anyway.

"The Colonel isn't going to like getting woken up," Avilova said. She lowered her rifle and stood beside it, the perfect image of a nighttime sentry. I followed suit, stationing myself at the opposite side of the door. In the glow of the lantern, we looked like angels of death. Or maybe demons.

"I don't think they'll wake him up just for her," I said. "She'll get as far as his aide, and then she'll be turned away. She'll be back before we wake up our relief."

We stood in silence for a moment before Avilova asked, "Did you ever come out here before? To visit your father?"

I snorted. "There's no way he'd have let me, even if I'd had the papers. And I knew it would have been a waste of time. He's too busy."

Avilova smirked. "I thought about trying it once, about a year ago. I was engaged to a doctor, and he told me there was a town where we could meet. I had it all planned out and was ready to get the tickets when the notice came."

She said it so casually that I almost didn't register it. "They shot a doctor?"

"It was a fever."

I'd been focused on munitions for so long, I'd forgotten the other ways people die in war. "I'm sorry," I said.

She looked down, digging the toe of her boot into the dirt. "It was a long time ago. Just a year, but also a lifetime. Do you know that Anna Akhmatova poem? The one that goes 'We aged a hundred years and this descended in just one hour'? That's what it feels like."

I didn't know the poem, but I wanted to.

"Wouldn't marriage have tied your suffragist plans into a knot?" I asked.

"Not marriage to him," she said softly. "It's odd, because a year ago I was ready to say my vows to him. Now, I've said them to Russia."

We were silent for a while, and then I asked, "I wonder what sort of Russia we'll go home to."

"It keeps changing, doesn't it? But it's all for the better. I believe that."

"Are you a socialist?"

"Most days. The socialists understand equality better than anyone else. But I think Lenin's a pompous ass."

I laughed. "Have you ever seen Lenin speak?"

"Once. That's all I could bear." We grinned at each other in the dark.

Another half hour went by and Bochkareva still had not returned. I couldn't stop yawning. We each chose a woman to replace us and settled into our spots. It turned out sleeping on planks of wood in Petrograd had been good training for the front.

In the morning, we found Bochkareva snoring on the bench. One of her eyes was swollen shut and her lip was split, but she was otherwise unhurt.

"What happened?" Alsu asked. Bochkareva smiled in her sleep.

"I think whatever she did worked," said Masha.

JULY 5, 1917

The week had gone by slowly. It rained often, which forced us to stay inside our meager quarters. The women fought like cornered dogs for the driest spots on the benches, but whenever a male soldier approached during meals, they were sisters-in-arms once again. When it wasn't raining, we drilled in full view of the male soldiers, who grew accustomed to our presence. The Colonel came to watch once and commended us, telling Bochkareva he'd never seen such a disciplined group of soldiers. The verbal abuses waned, and there were fewer and fewer physical attacks.

On the fifth night, Bochkareva relieved us of sentry duty.

"We have guards posted all around the encampment. The men know now it's not worth the risk to attack you again. Get some sleep. We'll be seeing action in a few days."

I made every member of my platoon lay her kit out. We divided up parts of each tent among six women. These would later roll up inside our greatcoats. For now, we needed our coats to sleep on. When we were cleaning the rifles, the smell of gun oil was so thick we had to take down the covers we'd placed over the broken windows to freshen the air.

Before I curled up for the night on my bench, I set my rifle beside the front door so that I could fall asleep with my eyes on it. Yellow light from the outside lamp filtered in through the thin weave of our makeshift curtains and lit a long strip along the edge of my bayonet.

The mud was knee-deep. A rifle in one hand and a Viking sword in the other. An arm sprouted from my back with a handful of grenades. The edge of a ruined field. I stepped out of the muck, pulled out my feet. I had chicken legs like Baba-Yaga. Ferocious, terrible, proud of it. Men hid in the trees. Shouting, telling me to lie down, to pull up my skirt, to run back home. I threw a grenade, blowing them to pieces. But the men did not leave. I threw all of my grenades. Then there was only one man left. He had two heads—one was Papa and the other was Maxim. "Go home! Be a peace-loving woman!" I raised the sword at Maxim's head. "Katyusha," he whispered. "I'm already dead."

No.

The door creaked shut.

I woke with a start, gasping for breath. Maxim and Papa's faces faded into the dream while I took stock of where I was. I was at the front. I was on the bench, and had my rifle by my—it was gone.

The spot by the door was empty. I rolled off the bench and felt along the floorboards, hoping it had only fallen over. But there was nothing there. I scratched at the darkness beneath my bench but only found my kit. The others were all asleep, and so I tiptoed around the room, trying to count the rifles lined up bayonet-to-butt in the weak yellow light. All accounted for. Except for mine.

Wedged into the doorframe at chest height was a bit of thick fabric. It was about the size of a playing card. I felt the embroidery and recognized it as a unit emblem, but I couldn't read it until I pushed it behind the makeshift curtain.

Tenth Army, Ninth Artillery Brigade.

My father's company.

JULY 6, 1917

My boots were damp. I had jammed my feet into them and the portyanki bunched unevenly, but it didn't matter now.

Bochkareva slept on the other side of the room, flat on her back. I gulped and made my way to her, each step like walking on glass. Someone had stolen my rifle, and it was my responsibility. My fault.

Half a meter from the bench, I snapped my heels together. "Sub-Lieutenant Bochkareva," I whispered.

Her eyes flicked open. "Pavlova. What's wrong?"

"Requesting permission to take an hour off." I gulped. "My rifle was just stolen."

She sat up, fluid as a jaguar. "You let someone steal your rifle?"

It didn't matter that I had been asleep. It was stupid to have left it by the door.

"Yes, Sub-Lieutenant."

She stood. There was a whoosh, and then her fist made contact with my jaw.

"Your rifle is your *life*, Pavlova! You gave it away!" she hissed. A few women began stirring on the benches, roused by the sound of our voices. "Muravyeva! Get over here."

Muravyeva stumbled over and fell into attention beside me. I looked down and saw she wore knit stockings over already-wrapped portyanki.

"Private Pavlova is temporarily relieved of duty. You are now Acting Leader of Third Platoon."

Muravyeva's breath hitched. "Yes, Sub-Lieutenant."

"Now get back to your bunk."

Muravyeva gave me a wide-eyed look before whirling around and climbing back onto the bench. Bochkareva sat back. "Go retrieve your rifle. Be back before the morning meal."

I nodded.

"But first," she said, and she fumbled with a pile of clean polishing cloths from beneath her spot on the bench. Then she unscrewed her canteen and dabbed at the cloth. "Here." She held it out to me.

The cloth was cool against my jaw.

———

I decided not to take the lantern.

Without my rifle, I was unburdened in the worst way. After a month of carrying it everywhere I went and a week needing it for personal protection, I felt naked.

It was a long kilometer to the Ninth Artillery encampment, along a farm road and through the woods. I walked in the grassy strip down the middle to avoid the worst of the mud, aware that I was alone. Bochkareva hadn't told me to bring anyone, which felt like a test. Out here, alone on the road and surrounded by flattened fields, I was as exposed as a lone tree in a lightning storm.

The dark woods lay spread out ahead, and I raced toward them. They could hold all sorts of monsters, but at least there I would not be out in the open, easy prey. My feet pounded the road, my chest heaved, and just as my lungs started to burn, I reached cover.

The pines were thick enough that nothing but needles and seedlings grew along the forest floor. The army, perhaps both armies, had walked a clear, wide path through the woods, and I kept to the edge, ready to jump behind a tree.

I'd been dreaming I was Baba-Yaga, the witch who ate the hearts of maidens. Those stories flashed in my mind, a screen of color and movement over the reality of a dark, empty wood. Hair by hair, my neck tickled and I wiped at it. I had been dreaming I was *her*, not her victim.

The forest should be afraid of *me*, I thought. After that the trees were no longer quite so dark, the cracking and shuffling sounds of moving creatures not so frightening. I was the monster creeping through the night woods.

The trees thinned and the path opened to a field. A city's worth of tents, crates of artillery shells, and the thin, wispy trails coming from iron cooking wagons filled the expanse. The sky glowed, spreading over the field in waves of rose and purple. And between the sky and the tents rose a bare flagpole erected beside a tiny wooden house wagon. The commander's quarters.

I'd always imagined my father's camp as something more substantial than this. He hadn't mentioned having to sleep like a circus performer. How had they all survived like this, winter after winter?

The answer was, of course, not *all* survived.

Surveying the camp, I realized it would be impossible to search all the tents or confront the men about my rifle. There was only one way to find it. Unfortunately, it rubbed my pride raw.

Throwing back my shoulders, I called out to the nearest tent.

"Ninth Artillery!"

Someone inside scrambled, and one of the men who'd been clustered near the cooking wagons trotted over. He paused when he saw me, his hand going to the rifle slung over his shoulder.

"Who's there?"

"Private Pavlova, from the Battalion of Death."

The man released his rifle and sauntered closer. "What do you want?"

"I need to speak with Colonel Pavlov."

He was close enough for me to see his features now. He wore a thick mustache and he hunched forward, bent at the mid-back. "It's early. What do you need to see him for?"

My stomach tightened into a knot. For days, I had known I would end up coming here somehow. I would have to see him, face him, and hear his sharp, breaking words.

"A private matter." When he still appeared skeptical, I gritted my teeth and added, "He's my father."

The soldier looked me over and nodded.

He led me around the tents, waving off questions from his comrades. Halfway to the wagon, the soldier saluted a second lieutenant who was carrying a tray of tea.

"Sir, this girl—uh, soldier—wants to speak with the colonel. She says he's her father."

The lieutenant halted. "Really? Are you Ekaterina Viktorovna?"

"Yes, sir."

"I've heard a lot about you over the years. Come with me."

So my father had spoken of me to his attaché, just as he'd written to me of this lieutenant. It felt oddly circular, and I wondered at the words, the descriptions, that had been passed between us all.

The lieutenant pointed at the wagon with the tea tray. "Does he know you're coming?"

"No."

"This is going to be the most interesting thing to happen all summer."

We walked over to the wagon. He climbed the two steps to the door and knocked.

"Come in," my father called, and his voice carried all my memories of him. Holding hands at marching parades, the black knight in chess swiping my white rook, and this growling voice of war merged into a shadow that was both familiar and foreign.

The lieutenant ducked inside. "Sir, you have a visitor."

I scraped the mud off my boots on a nearby rock and climbed the steps to join him. There wasn't much space inside the wagon. My father sat on a cane chair between a mattress and a table, which held the tea tray and two lit candles. Dark circles hung from my father's washed-out blue eyes, but his uniform was impeccable. His mustache was no longer the rough gray of my childhood, but drained of color, as white as bones.

Before the lieutenant could introduce me, I saluted. "Colonel Pavlov."

His teacup rattled on the saucer. "Ekaterina?"

The look on his face was almost worth the cost of losing my rifle. He quickly recovered, but it was enough. His normally serene facade had cracked, something I hadn't seen since my mother left.

"Lieutenant Sarkovsky, that will be all."

The lieutenant gave me an encouraging smile as he stepped back out into the fresh air. When the door shut behind him, the candle flames flickered.

I stole a glance at the wall behind my father. A calendar hung from a nail, and beside that was a framed family photo. I didn't have to look long to know every detail, because the copy was in the dining room at home. I was fourteen, still in braids. Maxim's shoulders were thin. Babushka was gripping the front of her blouse like it was trying to fly open. And my father's eyes were calm, proud, and eternal.

"Hello, Papa."

"Do you have permission to visit?" he asked. He set his teacup on the tray and brushed off his chest, wiping away non-existent crumbs.

"My commander knows I'm here." I gulped.

"You completed your training." It wasn't a question. "Successfully, I heard."

"So did you," I said before I could think better of it.

He blinked. "I had no choice, back when I was your age. It was either join the army or starve on the streets. But you had a choice."

He picked up his teacup and took another sip. "I know why they formed this women's battalion, and I understand it," he said. "I even support the idea behind it—to rally the men and get them back on the field. But you . . ." he studied my mud-encrusted boots, the skull-and-crossbones sewed onto my sleeve, and my short-cropped hair. "You don't have to do this."

"I couldn't stay behind any longer, Papa. And I would have made a terrible nurse."

Ten years ago, my father would've chuckled at that. I couldn't remember the last time I'd made him laugh. I certainly wasn't going to manage it today.

"Why are you here?" he asked brusquely.

"My rifle was stolen in the night."

He settled his teacup back onto its saucer. "And you believe I will help you recover it," he said.

His tone was a punch to the stomach. "I did. But if I was wrong, then I won't waste any more of your time. I'll go find it amongst your men. On my own."

"Amongst *my men*?"

I ripped the Ninth Artillery Brigade patch from my pocket and waved it in the air. "The person who stole my rifle left this behind, wedged into our barracks door."

"Let me see." The arrogance and pride had drained out of his voice.

When I handed it over, he squinted and cursed, and I realized he hadn't been able to see it from across the small space. My father was losing his vision.

"Either someone planted this as a decoy, or one of my soldiers does have your rifle and left this behind as a boast."

The vibrant father I remembered returned. His face reddened, and he stood up, no longer looking his age. "I will see to it. You'll need it."

He meant I would need it in battle. My heart beat faster at the thought of it. "Thank you."

The crease between his brows softened. Suddenly, part of me wanted to sit with him and hear the stories of the saints, his versions always more vivid than those in the books. But all that was as long gone as the color in his hair.

"You should get back to your camp," he croaked. I was halfway to the door again before he laid a hand on my shoulder. The weight of it was nothing to the years of disappointment, years of abandonment. "The uniform suits you. You look like a soldier."

"I *am* a soldier," I said, but I was still turned away from him. "And I won't run away."

"I know." He squeezed my shoulder and spoke into my cap. "But don't let yourself get captured, Katya. Do you understand what I'm saying?

Here was my Papa, the one who'd told me bedtime stories of Saint Olga, the vengeful, brave queen of Old Russia. Fluidly, I reached inside my shirt and pulled out the vial of cyanide we'd been issued in case of capture. It whispered of endings as it dangled on its cord.

"I won't, Papa."

"What happened to Prince Mal?"

"He went up in flames."

"For certain? What if he escaped?"

"That, my dear, is for another night."

"Isn't there a moral? You always give a moral."

"To Olga's revenge? I suppose the moral is: don't try to take the son of a Russian woman."

"But the Tsar does that. He takes peasant boys and makes them be soldiers."

"Don't talk of the Tsar like that."

"I know a better one: if you don't want to lose your family, do something about it."

16

JULY 7, 1917

BACK at my encampment, I found Bochkareva watching Liddikova's platoon practice field maneuvers, leaning against a wooden fence that had once been a pen for animals but was now missing three sides. She turned her head as I approached.

"Pavlova."

"Sub-Lieutenant."

She shielded her eyes from the sun. "You returned without a rifle."

"Colonel Pavlov said he would have it sent here," I said.

"When you get it back, you can have your platoon," she muttered. "Muravyeva is doing her best, but they don't listen to her as quickly as they do to you. Now get inside. They're in there, taking a break."

I saluted and ran inside.

I found half my platoon lounging on their sleeping benches in various levels of disarray after their morning exercises. They looked up, and Muravyeva shouted my name. The others chorused, "Oo-rah!"

Then Dubrovskaya tripped over someone's boots and was caught by two others. In the fall, her unbelted trousers slipped and we all got a glimpse of her bare backside. My soldiers laughed, her most of all. There were some giggles, someone slapped her on the rump, and she pulled up her trousers a bit too fast. One of the offending boots skidded against the door.

Masha picked it up, laughed, and lobbed it back at the cluster of women on the floor.

We were all laughing now. These were my comrades, my sisters-in-arms, my soldiers. My brother's desertion still beat like an extra heart in my chest, but here was a platoon full of women who would not flee. Who were ready to fight. Who would stand for Russia. With me.

———

That afternoon, an officer made his way down the farm road from the forest. We could see his form grow larger the closer he got, and by the time he arrived, the women were placing bets on who he'd come for. When he got close enough, I saw that he was carrying two rifles, and one was a little shorter than the other.

"Lieutenant Sarkovsky," I said, standing.

He brightened when we made eye contact. "Private Pavlova. I brought something for you." A few of the women giggled, and he cleared his throat. "From Colonel Pavlov."

"Thank you, sir." I clambered over the women sitting between us and gave him a quick salute.

He separated the two rifles' straps and handed me the shorter one. The moment it fell into my palm, I knew it was mine, but I checked the serial number to be sure. It was right, it was back, it was home. Then the lieutenant reached into a leather pouch hanging from his belt and pulled out a newspaper-wrapped package. "And this is for you too."

"Thank you." The package was light and fit snugly in one of my palms.

"You're welcome." He looked around at the women, who were staring openly at our exchange. "They found the men who took it. They're being sentenced right now." When I winced, he added solemnly, "It's unlawful to steal a comrade's weapon. You shouldn't worry about them. They were trying to sabotage your battalion, one person at a time, but their plans have been ruined. Are you making the next advance? With the others?"

I crossed my arms, holding the packet close. "Of course."

"Then I wish you speed and strength. The artillery will be there clearing the way for you."

"Speed and strength to you too, sir."

With a tap at his cap, he turned and marched off before I could salute him again.

I sat down on a nearby log, holding the package in one arm and my rifle in the other.

"Is that from your father?" Masha asked, sitting beside me. I nodded but didn't say anything.

It was strange: He hadn't sent me a package in years. It was unlike him to do anything more than was required, even for family. "You have to open it now. If you don't . . ." Masha didn't finish her sentence, but I knew what she meant. If I didn't open it now, I might not get another chance.

Quickly, I unfolded the paper and laid it flat. In the center lay a tiny painted icon framed in gold leaf and birch bark.

I brushed a finger over the face on the icon. I knew what this was. It had been mine once, but it had been missing for years. I never thought I'd see it again.

"Which saint is that?" Masha asked, leaning over my lap, not seeing my tears.

"It's Saint Olga."

She pulled back. "The one who sent all those birds with flaming sticks to burn down the enemy town? The one he mentioned in the telegram and said you're nothing like?"

I wiped the tears from my face, then pressed my cold palms against my cheeks. "Yes. But it's more than that. When I was eight, my parents were fighting a lot. After the shouting and the door-slamming died down, Papa would come to my room and tell me stories to help me sleep." I traced the icon's edge with a fingernail. It was not a delicate little icon. It was thick, the image painted directly on the wood. Beautiful and strong.

"One night he told me a story about a very brave woman. Olga. He always told me battle stories. A story about avenging the death of a king, of Saint Georgi and the dragon, of using one's wits to outsmart Baba-Yaga. But this time, it was a story about a woman. I told him I wanted to be like Olga when I grew up." My lips were salty. "Then he said, 'Hopefully not as bloodthirsty.'"

"Let me see it. I've never held one so small."

While she admired it, I thought of what had happened a few days after Papa told me that story. Mama ran off with her lover. Babushka told Maxim and me that we must be brave, that we must support each other while she was gone. We never heard from Mama, and Papa never spoke of her again. And he never told me another bedtime story.

Masha handed back the icon. "You've got to keep it on you so Saint Olga can go with you into battle."

"Yes. I think that's why he sent it." He must have taken it with him when he left for the front. Had he taken it to think of me, or to give himself strength?

"He sent it," said Masha, "because you're here to avenge Russia. You're here to fight like Olga. And he knows it. He *approves*."

While I was sewing a bag for the icon to wear around my neck, I happened to glance again at the newspaper my father had wrapped it in. I hadn't read the news in a week and had no idea what had been going on. Life at the front felt frozen, as though we were in a snow globe, protected from and yet shaken by all that happened around us.

The page was from the *Novoe Vremia*, the paper I'd grown up handing to my father in exchange for a pat on the head. Lazily, I scanned the headlines, hoping to get my mind off the war for just one moment. Then I stopped and read a headline twice.

Bolsheviks Attempt Coup; Many Arrested; Lenin on the Run.

The article explained that a few days earlier, the Bolsheviks had attempted to overrun the Provisional Government. Their attempts failed, partly because there was new evidence that Lenin had been receiving money from the German government in exchange for attempting to end Russia's involvement in the war. Many Bolsheviks were arrested, including one of the leaders, Trotsky. Lenin, however, escaped.

I read through the list of published names and found what

I had been looking for: Sergei Fyodorovich Grigorev. He was in prison.

I felt queasy. Although he and I had often disagreed, I had never wished him any harm. He was a scholar, a chemistry student, an idealist—not a common criminal. Carefully, I cut his name out of the newspaper with the tip of my knife. Then, with a dab of wax from a nearby candle, I stuck it to the back of the icon.

Perhaps St. Olga would keep us both safe from harm. After all, we were both fighting for a Russia we believed in.

JULY 8, 1917

We circled around Bochkareva after dinner, some kneeling on the dirt while others just sat, knees gathered to their chests, rifles strapped to our backs. We looked ready for battle. And we were. Gone were the factory girls, students, and political idealists.

No one whispered, no one giggled, and above all, no one could look away from Bochkareva. She paced inside our circle like a tiger ready to pounce. She gripped the hilt of her saber, rubbing her thumb over the golden pommel. Her other hand rested on the pistol. Both were signs of her new rank and responsibilities.

"We will get into our places at 0300," she said. "The sun will rise at 0340. The call to attack will come shortly before that. Your platoon leaders will give you more precise orders." I felt dozens of eyes on me like a wave of heat.

Bochkareva led us in prayer, and while everyone bowed their heads, I peeked. Avilova met my gaze, and although the corner of her mouth threatened to turn up, her brow remained serious. *Yes*, she seemed to say, *eyes on the enemy, not on God.*

We'd strengthened our bodies and minds, we'd learned to shoot, to crawl, to stab, and religion took no part in it other than to give us its blessing. We were fighting for Russia, not for God.

I imagined what the other side might be doing in that same moment. A circle of soldiers receiving orders for battle from their commander, kneeling in prayer and kissing their German crosses.

I blinked away the image.

After the prayer, Bochkareva ordered us to split into our platoons. I rolled my shoulders and walked to the side of the barracks to meet my women. They came in twos and threes, broken off into the little groups that had formed during our training and our journey to the front. Muravyeva brought her rifle to attention before me.

"All present, Private Pavlova," she said. Then she added, quietly, "I'm honored to fight with you."

If we could win on serious faces alone, Muravyeva would save the war.

"It's my honor, with you."

I took the deepest, slowest breath I could manage, hoping it would calm my nerves. Then I lifted my chin and looked out at my soldiers. "Depending on how you look at it, we were given either the best or the worst assignment."

"What do you mean?" someone in the back asked. We stood in the shade, and I couldn't make out the faces clearly that far back.

"We've got the central position. And we're going first. The First Platoon has the left flank, we'll be in the center. The other two will be coming up on our right, but not until the first pause in the attack." No one swayed on her feet, which I took as a good sign. Using a stick, I scratched out the plan on the ground. "I'll take you forward, to this point." I made an X. "The goal is to get past their defenses before their reinforcements arrive. According to the major's intelligence, they are undermanned here. If we can get there and hold our position, Third Platoon will come in from the right with reinforcements."

"What about the rest of the Tenth Army?" This came from Alsu.

"They'll be with us. We have two male platoons going with us, so we won't be alone." There was an audible sigh of relief from at least half the women. "But even without them, we could do it. It's only a hundred meters."

"Open field?" Muravyeva asked.

I dug the stick deeper into the dirt. "Barbed wire, mines, and three trenches."

"At least she's honest," came a reply.

"We'll make it," I said, looking up sharply at the woman who'd made the joke. "We're the sharpest battalion around here. You've seen the men! That's what the enemy will be expecting. They won't be expecting precision. They're expecting a band of soldiers who turn tail and run back to the woods at the first sight of a mortar. They won't expect *us*." With a kick, I cleared my scratches in the dirt.

Masha laughed. "Well, they certainly aren't expecting a platoon of women."

Later, when all was dark and no one could sleep, I reached out and gently tapped Masha's head.

"I know I shouldn't say it, but I'm afraid," I whispered.

"It's war, Katya," she whispered back. "We're all going to face our demons tomorrow."

My particular demon was a dark, hidden thing I didn't want brought into the light, but at this moment, it seemed the right thing to do. "I'm afraid that when we get out there tomorrow, when everything is bullets and bayonets, I'll forget everything we've learned and fail our platoon. I'm not afraid of dying. I'm afraid of being a coward."

She laughed quietly. "You're not a coward."

"How do you know?"

"I know you. And I trust you."

I reached for one of her hands and squeezed her fingers tight. "If anything happens to me, promise you'll take the icon?"

"No. Because you'll survive, Katya. I know it."

I sighed. "Well, if you won't accept Saint Olga's protection, I suppose I'll just have to—"

"If you tell me you're going to watch out for me, I'll be the first to take a shot at you, Katya. I can take care of myself. When we make our attack, we will do what we were trained to do. Because that's what we're here for."

I slid my free hand into the little bag where I had stashed Saint Olga. "All right. Tomorrow we're warriors."

"We already are. Now stop talking. We need to sleep now."

As I tried to fall asleep, my mind ran all over the place—my father's cabin, Maxim joking about using the umbrella in battle, imaginary German soldiers kneeling in prayer, and Sergei in a prison in Petrograd. I thought of my mother and how she'd left without saying goodbye. I thought of Babushka, who'd believed so fervently in prayer. Above all I thought of Saint Olga. I held the icon to my chest and gently rubbed the bit of gold overlay, trying to memorize the feel of it, remembering the story of Olga's revenge.

Despite my earlier thoughts on religion and war, I drifted off to sleep with Olga's prayer on my lips.

Saint Olga, help us overcome the world.

17

JULY 9, 1917
SMORGON, BELARUS

IT was almost time.

I slid the bolt back. *Click.* I stuck the cartridge in the chamber and pushed the bolt forward. *Click.* A shiver crept down my arms. It had nothing to do with the night chill and everything to do with the fact that I was deep in a trench, knees pressed against the wooden planks lining the earthen walls.

It turned out that trenches weren't straight furrows in the ground. They zigged and zagged, and doubled back. They had alcoves and piles of ammunition. This particular one housed a machine gun and crew, protected from the opposing gunfire by nothing more than spare logs and bags of sand. The longer I sat here, the more I realized the protection built into the trench was artificial, offering only the illusion of safety.

I shifted on my feet, and the leather in my boots squeaked. They were damp, but not soaking. Word came down the trench and it seemed my platoon had the driest bit. It was a fair trade, I thought, since so far we'd done nothing more than crouch in the dark, waiting for the call to attack.

Masha and Alsu were nearby. I made sure of it. Not only

did I feel the need to keep them safe, but Masha's skill with a rifle wasn't something I wanted to ignore and Alsu had a sixth sense when it came to hand-to-hand combat. Yes, I favored them, but this could be our last day. I would take every moment that I could.

It was still dark, but the sun would come soon. According to Bochkareva, who had been running up and down our mile-long portion checking on us, we would attack before first light. That meant sometime within the next fifteen minutes, judging by the way the eastern sky was starting to pale.

My toes had gone numb, and I shifted my weight. Masha coughed into her sleeve.

"Any minute now," I whispered.

Down the line, I could hear Bochkareva shouting something, but it wasn't the call to attack. "Alsu, take a look," I said, and Alsu climbed up the ladder, step by careful step, and peeked. "Anything up there?"

She ducked down. "Nothing. But I see lights moving. The enemy's first line isn't that far away."

I nodded. "One hundred meters."

"An easy sprint," Masha said softly. She grinned, but it was more of a grimace. That was as it should be. Here and now, Masha was supposed to look like a killer. We all were.

Alsu peeked again, then came down the ladder with a quiet jump. Her rifle butt smacked against the last two wooden planks on the wall, and I cringed. "Lots of barbed wire, too, but some of it looks like it's been cut."

"Nothing we haven't gone through before," I said. I didn't say that the last time was at home, in daylight, without anyone shooting at us. They didn't need that reminder.

Masha tugged on her cap, settling it straight in the middle

of her face and scratching at her shorn hair. I could feel her nerves reverberating against mine, which had been humming, louder and louder, like the rails just before a train comes screaming into the station. It was surprising that the enemy couldn't sense us solely by this buzzing of energy thickening the trenches. It had a certain smell, sharp and metallic, mixed with urine and sweat. I wrinkled my nose.

"Pavlova!" It was Bochkareva. She ran from behind a corner, her face red and angry, and I stood up straight, ignoring the tingling in my toes. "They've made the call for attack." There was a noticeable lack of yelling, shooting, and artillery barrage, and I raised my eyebrow at her. "But the men refuse to go."

My stomach plummeted. "All of them?"

"Three regiments are ignoring the order and have convened to discuss the risks. They've made a committee."

I frowned, thinking this was just as Sergei would have wanted it. But it hardly seemed practical right now.

"This is why I forbid Order Number One in my ranks. Because when it comes time to make an advance, we can't have the troops stopping to talk about it over cups of tea!" She was spitting, and I resisted the urge to step back from the drops of anger spraying in the air. "A committee! What the hell are we doing here, if it's not to fight? Are we supposed to just let the Germans skip into Russia?"

"Are there any regiments that *will* attack?" I asked, trying to calm her.

"Ours. Some men from the 525th. Also your father's unit, so we have some artillery." She paused. "We could still do it."

"How long will the committee discuss this?"

She frowned and rubbed at her right hip. "Hours. I've heard they'll argue until it's too light out to make an advance."

"They don't want to be here," I said. "They wouldn't be effective anyway."

She nodded briskly. "I'll be back in a minute. Get your women ready."

———

"Pavlova," Masha asked a few minutes later, "how many are there?"

"Of us?"

"The Germans."

"Eighteen battalions." I checked my pouches and counted the grenades I've loaded onto my body. None of them were gas, but they were all from my factory. *My* grenades.

"Eighteen!" Alsu gasped. "How can we possibly survive?"

A handful of other women clumped around us, drawn to our section by Bochkareva's earlier presence. They were all from my platoon. My women. My responsibility. The smell of fear was stronger now, and I blew out a quick, hard breath to get rid of it. I had to rally them.

"It sounds as though they have the advantage, but they do not." I paused and waited until they settled, then raised my voice. "We have several advantages, actually. One, we have the element of surprise. Sure, they expect an attack any day now, but they don't know for sure it's today. And they don't know that three hundred Amazons will be descending upon them before the sun rises."

This garnered a few nervous smiles.

"Second, we have them outnumbered. Yes, some of the men have refused. They're scared and they're tired. They've been doing this far longer than we have. But I don't think they'll abandon us. If we go forth, they will follow. It's what we came here for, isn't it? Sometimes all it takes is *one* woman. Did Saint Olga turn Russia over to her enemies? No! She fought. She *burned them to the ground.*"

Several women silently raised their fists in the air. Their faces were shining, full of power. My voice grew stronger.

"And third, when has a European army *ever* succeeded in an invasion of Russia? Never! Those men on the other side of the wire know this. They *know* they're fighting a useless war. They *know* history is on our side. Because Russian men—and women—never give up. Our men may get a little scared once in a while," and I flashed the brightest smile left in my arsenal, "but they're proud. And they sure as hell aren't going to let us show the world that we're stronger, braver, and better trained than they are. They'll follow us into that forest, and then after we're done with this war, they'll say it was their idea all along."

Alsu laughed, agreeing.

"So we have the advantage. Just think of the Germans' faces when they realize they've lost to women!"

My heart was beating so hard it nearly made its way up my throat. The tension was a little looser, but I could still sense the humming, that train that's coming in full speed.

Suddenly Bochkareva was back, running along the line. "Five minutes!" she shouted at us. "Remember: don't be cowards! You are soldier women!" Then she was past me and running down the trench to Avilova's platoon.

A few minutes later, a whistling sound jolted us to attention. A mortar, flying over our heads toward the enemy trenches, joined a moment later by a dozen or so more. My father's unit was pounding the enemy.

It was time.

"Go!" I shouted. We climbed up out of the ground like angry ants, and by the light of artillery explosions raced across the open land, screaming at the top of our lungs.

"Ooh-rahhhhhhhh!"

Masha was to my left and Alsu to my right. We sprinted together, our rifles out front and ready, nearly as long as we were. Exploding dirt and sand shot into the air like geysers, spraying the field with rocks and debris, and still we ran on.

There was a flash of white to the west, and I saw our standard bearer, Dubrovskaya, running along with the flag of our battalion. It whipped in the air, backlit by the orange glow of fire and the white flash of explosion.

The barbed wire had been cut, so we didn't have to crawl under it. I jumped over the remnants on the ground, scraped my knee, and kept running. We were halfway to the first line when the enemy poured out of their trench. They were giants. Armed giants with rounded metal helmets. There was no cover, so I took aim.

Three of them fell backwards into the trench before I'd even taken my first shot. Masha pulled her bolt back and forth, shooting as she ran, and even though the air around me erupted in pops and spraying earth, for a split second I saw her like I'd never seen her before. She was too quick with her rifle to be human. Her cheeks were glowing in the unnatural light and her eyes were focused and deadly. She was an angel of death, a Valkyrie, and I realized she could truly hold her own. She was carrying the blood of Russia in her veins; she wasn't going to lie down and let these men walk over her.

There was another pop beside me and the moment disappeared. A man ran at me, and my chest beat in panic before I took aim and pulled the trigger. He stumbled, but he wasn't down. I hit him in the shoulder. His eyes were a light blue, so pale they were almost white, and time seemed to both slow down and speed up. He rushed at me, his irises shrinking to little points, and raised his weapon. Two thoughts crossed my mind in the five steps he took. One, I didn't have time to put another bullet in the chamber, and two, he wasn't going to shoot me. He was going to stab. His jaw clenched, and his teeth shone bright, but it wasn't a sneer.

It was the smile of death.

I held my rifle out and lunged to the left. He missed, but I did not. My bayonet slid in beneath his ribs but met with more resistance than I'd expected. I had to push, slamming my whole body into him. His breath was hot on my forehead and he screamed. When he fell, I landed on top of him. My rifle was stuck in the mud beneath his body, because I'd stabbed him through. I scrambled to my feet and yanked the blade out of him. He gurgled, but I didn't look.

Kneeling, I vomited. I had to forget how it felt to push into him. I had to forget, but all I could feel was the pressure in my hands, the weight of the weapon, the heaviness of his body, and then out of the corner of my eye, I saw red coming from his mouth. It matched the tint on the end of my bayonet.

A large drop of blood slid down the sharpened edge, but I didn't stand there to watch it fall. Wiping my mouth, I jumped back up because there were more of them and I couldn't see Masha anywhere.

I pulled the bolt back and set the next bullet in place. I didn't want to be caught like that again. Then I ran. The buzzing I had felt earlier was pulsing, strong as my heart, through every limb in my body. I was alive, and everything was sharper. The sounds ricocheted in my ears, the colors were as bright as midday, and I could smell all of it. The blood, the dew, the metallic tang of iron and steel. It billowed around me, and I cut through it like a knife.

The screams turned to grunts as the others slammed into the enemy. Some of the women went down, but we were fresh and well trained. More of the men fell than we did. And then we were climbing into their trench.

"Holy Mother of God!" Masha screamed in my ear. She grabbed me around the neck and I couldn't tell if she was sobbing or laughing. I wasn't even sure I could peel those two actions apart at this point. "We made it."

I squeezed her, and then pulled back. She was splattered in blood.

"It's not mine, I swear."

I took a look at the other women. We only had a few seconds before we needed to move. I would have counted them, but there were too many. It was a good thing.

"Lomonosova, take three and head down that way." I gestured east, down the trench. "Take out anyone you see. Muravyeva, you take three and go the opposite. Same orders." The women nodded in agreement and ran down the enemy trench. Seconds later, there was an explosion, but someone called back that Muravyeva's group was fine.

It took longer than it should have to clear the trench. We took no prisoners, because whoever didn't fight us had crawled back to the second trench, closer to the trees.

The sounds of artillery continued, popping and booming in the background. They'd changed their angle and were shooting deeper into the enemy lines, almost to the forest line. They must know we'd made it this far. Alsu covered her ears with her hands, but her eyes were clear. She wasn't as far gone to shock as some of the others.

"Anyone not make it?" I asked her.

She nodded. "Dubrovskaya."

The standard-bearer. She'd begged to carry the colors, saying it would be her honor. And it had been her death.

"Who has it now?" I asked, meaning the standard.

"Tsvetkova."

"All right." I shouted at the others to get their attention. "Hey! We can't stop now."

The fear on their faces had evolved. Before, it had been vague, but now it held an echo of what we'd run through. This fear was specific. It was the whoosh of air as a bullet missed and the spray of dirt in your eyes. It was knowing you didn't have time to pull back the bolt. It was the tremendous force it took to stab a man through the ribs. It was a demon on our shoulders, digging its nails through the epaulets.

"Sisters!" I shouted. "We go again!"

Then, even though I was so nervous I wasn't sure I'd be able to aim at anything but the sun, I crawled up a ladder and hit the ground running. My platoon was strong, fearless, and persistent, and they didn't leave me there alone for long.

This time, the enemy was ready. They lobbed grenades, which I leapt over, counting seconds and meters of effective range. They were simple explosives, not gas, and I focused on this while I ran. My lungs burned. I was still breathing.

The nearer I got to the second trench, the more focused I became. My vision was clear and bright straight ahead. A man came into view and I shot. He fell; I'd gotten him in the chest. I reached into my bag, grabbed a grenade, and pulled the pin. Then I took a balancing step back and let it fly.

It arced gracefully and landed in the trench. There was a shout of alarm, then a boom. Wood splinters and dirt shot in the air but I didn't duck, I didn't even pause. I ran to the edge and leapt down into the trench. I took my first look after I'd already committed and landed on the body of a man. He was wet with blood so warm it felt like a bath. I rolled off just as my platoon landed down around me.

We'd taken the second trench.

"Here." Masha handed me a handkerchief she'd pulled out of a hidden pocket in her tunic. "That was hell on earth."

I snorted in response, because I couldn't talk while wiping blood off my lips. I didn't want to taste the blood of a German.

"I think we need you to throw more grenades next time," she continued. "Can you get them all the way across the next field? It'd save some ammo."

"Very funny," I muttered. I wiped my forehead and my neck, and then tossed the handkerchief to the ground. There was no point in giving it back. One glance down at my chest and I knew there was nothing to be done for the rest of me. I'd have to wear this man's blood until we were done.

An order came down the line from Bochkareva. We were to wait here because the men were forming up behind us. How she could possibly know this, I had no idea, but I welcomed the respite. We cleared out the rest of the trench within a few minutes, again finding very few men left. There was a shout somewhere to the east, followed by a series of pops, and then it was over. Another man down, I thought, because I wouldn't allow it to be one of us.

One of the women—Pul'khova—crumpled against the wall with a loud sob. I ran over thinking she must be wounded, but she waved me off. She bit on her knuckles, seemingly unaware or uncaring that her hands were mottled with scrapes and dirt. Tears streamed down her cheeks.

I knelt beside her. "We're going to rest now."

"I did it." Her words were almost too quiet, but I knew what she said. "I did it."

"Yes, you did it. We all did."

Her eyes darted around, like she'd just realized someone was talking to her and couldn't find the source of my voice. "I sliced his throat." That explained the red streaks across her arms.

"If you hadn't, you'd be dead."

Alsu came to her other side and wrapped an arm around her while taking the fist out of Pul'khova's mouth. It was something I should have done but hadn't thought about. "Shh, Nastya, shh. We're here. We're almost done." Carefully she pulled Pul'khova's canteen off its strap, opened it, and held it to the woman's mouth. Water trickled down her chin.

We were all different. A few women looked less stricken than others, but the shadows were still there.

Bochkareva arrived, dragging her leg. It was the one she'd damaged the year before. "How many casualties?" she asked.

I pulled myself onto my feet. "I'm not sure."

"Well make sure, dammit!" Then she was gone again, leaving a line in the dirt behind her as she went.

After counting, I almost wanted to join Pul'khova. We'd lost two from the Third Platoon. "Only two," Masha said. But they were gone forever. Their bodies were still out there behind us, breadcrumbs left behind on our trail into horror.

"Gubina," I said to Masha, gesturing at the crates stacked up against the walls. "Go find out if there's any ammo here we can take with us. I'm almost out of cartridges."

We waited for hours. There was no sign that our men were coming, but there wasn't any retaliation from the Germans, either. We bandaged ourselves up, took stock of ammunition, and, for those of us able to keep anything down, ate whatever food we found that the Germans had left behind. We dragged the enemy bodies to the side and piled them on top of one another. Someone found the bloody handkerchief and laid it on top of the bodies like she was marking the spot. Bright red. Dead.

"I think we're going to make it," Masha said. "Your speech worked."

I blinked. "My speech?"

She bumped her shoulder into mine and a memory broke over me, one of sunshine and fountains, braids and girlish laughter. There was no laughter anymore. "Sure," she said. "You inspired everyone. Sisters-in-arms. How we have the advantage. All of it. You were right. They weren't ready." Her eyes flattened. "It's not something I want to do every day, you know. Just until it's all over. Just until the Germans are gone."

I suppressed a yawn and leaned back against the dirt wall of the trench. "Have you seen any of your papers yet?"

"I think so. It's hard to tell if I was the one who packed it or not. I should have signed them."

For a second, I forgot the smell of blood. "I'm not sure that would have helped your quotas."

"Have you seen any of your grenades?"

"They're not *my* grenades. But yes." I waved at the space around us. "That's what I used to clear out this trench."

"What about the gas ones?"

"Those haven't made it out to the front yet, it seems. Not here, anyway." I tapped my gas mask, which I'd affixed to my waistband. It stared up at me, empty-eyed and gruesome as a grasshopper. Maxim started to encroach on my mind, and I pushed him away. "Masha," I began, then realized I didn't know what to say. We were deep into the enemy's trenches, covered in blood. My ears still rang from the grenade and all the rounds I'd spent crossing no man's land. The back of my mind was drowning in blood and screams, but we were alive. "You're the best friend I've ever had."

"I know." She smiled, then stretched one leg out and let her boot roll outward, relaxed. "Us against the world, right?"

"Us against the world."

Something whistled and we all looked up. There was no time. Our trench was barraged by mortars that sank into the mud before bursting into green clouds.

"Gas! Gas!" someone screamed.

Masha and I jumped apart and wrestled with the straps holding our masks to our thighs. My fingers shook, and I kept fumbling. Masha reached over and sliced through my strap with a knife she'd pulled from her boot. I slipped the mask on over my head—no time to even register my surprise. Our caps fell to the ground like leaves blown off trees in a storm.

We moved mechanically, just as we'd practiced. I twisted the canister on tightly and breathed through it. The air was thick as fog, but tinted green. Poison. I wracked my brain, but I couldn't remember the name of this gas. I couldn't remember what it did, or how long it remained in the air. My skin tingled, but it didn't sting.

"They're coming!" someone shouted, but her voice was rubbery. I pulled myself together. If they'd sent us a volley of gas, they'd be on the ground already. I grabbed Masha's hand and together we made our way to the ladders.

"Third Platoon, go!" I shouted, but the sound was muffled. I was commanding my troops in a soup, but I didn't really need to say anything. This was our third time, and we all knew what to do. We crawled up and ran.

Fighting in a cloud was an entirely different monster. We were creatures crawling out of the sludge. The enemy wore masks, and somehow this made it easier. I couldn't see their teeth as they grimaced, their eyes hidden behind circles of glass. We fought in a storm of green. It was a nightmare, but real.

Someone went down beside me, but I didn't look. I lobbed grenades, one after the other, and kept moving forward. I picked grenades off the fallen and tossed those too. They were German, but they worked as well as mine.

Out of the green fog, a rifle butt smacked into my head. I fell sideways. A man loomed over me, fumbling with a revolver. His rifle must have been empty. I picked up my rifle, aimed, and shot. He jumped in the air, then fell onto my bayonet. He was a thin man, but the blade didn't go all the way through. I kicked him off of me and tried to stand, but my head was spinning. I clutched the side of my face and felt at where the buckle of my gas mask cut into my temple. It was wet.

Wiping at the lenses, I squinted until I could see the scar in the earth that marked the next trench. It cut through before the first line of trees, maybe fifty more meters.

"Katya!" Masha swooped down and pulled on me. "Don't stop!"

I was dizzy. I was going to vomit again, but I couldn't do that in my mask. And I couldn't take the mask off. I bit at my tongue and let her drag me along.

"Not far," she grunted, then hauled me onto my feet. "Get moving, Pavlova!"

My father wouldn't have stayed here. I took a few steps. Pulled the bolt back on my rifle and got it ready.

There were a series of pops. Machine gun fire. It sent the dirt up in a line like a strip of firecrackers.

Masha stumbled.

"Masha!" I screamed. I scanned the trees where the machine fire was coming from, took in the holes scattered across her thighs, and then sent the gunners a gift I packed back in Petrograd. I waited 3.5 seconds, and then everyone within three meters of the machine gun was gone.

My ears roared. I lifted Masha onto my back, barely registering the hard shape of her rifle digging into my spine, and ran. I couldn't shoot, but I didn't care. I carried her forward, pausing for a moment to throw another grenade into the trench, and when the air cleared, I set her onto the edge. I crawled down, then paused halfway down the ladder to pull her into my arms, and together we fell.

There was too much blood. When I pulled off my mask, I saw it. I knew it, but I couldn't accept it.

"Oh, Masha," I choked, pulling her overcoat off her shoulder and pressing it against the bullet holes. There were too many. Her legs were a sieve and she was draining right through them. I tugged off her mask and threw it to the side. "Someone! I need a tourniquet!"

Alsu placed her hand on my shoulder, shaking her head. It wouldn't help.

"I wasn't afraid," she whispered. "Still not." Her hand flapped in the air and I took it, squeezing her palm in mine.

The shooting stopped but the nightmare continued.

She closed her eyes, and I wanted to pull them open, to see her seeing me. "Masha! Wake up!" I shook her, but her neck was weak and her head hit the ground. "You can't die, Masha. You can't!" I cried into her face, filling the hollow space at the corner of her mouth with my tears. "No! No. No."

There was a sudden chill, like someone had opened a window in winter and all the warm air rushed out of the crack, and that was how I knew she'd gone.

Someone pulled on my arm, but I shook her off and clung to Masha's body. Then I sobbed, because it wasn't Masha anymore.

"Get up, Pavlova." Bochkareva yanked me up off the ground. I turned to yell at her, but she was crying too, and the shock of seeing tears on her face stopped me. "We have to move."

"We can't leave her here!"

"She's dead. I'm sorry, but she's dead and we are still alive. We have to clear our position. You're a platoon leader, Pavlova! You can't sit here by your dead friend. There will be time later to grieve."

I pulled out of Bochkareva's sizable arms and knelt back down beside Masha. She was gone, but I whispered the words anyway. "I won't be afraid, Masha. I'll be fierce. Forever."

Then I got back on my feet and wiped my face with the back of my hands.

"Good girl," Bochkareva said. "Get your women accounted

for and clear the western portion. We'll wait here until reinforcements come."

I struggled to think through what she'd just said. "Reinforcements?"

She shot me an impatient look and spoke with more emphasis. "I'm sending a report and asking for reinforcements. We've almost got this area taken, per orders. Surely the men will come now that we've done all the hard work."

If the men had been with us, things might have been different. I faced my troops and relayed Bochkareva's orders. When I turned back, our leader was gone but there was a crisp, clean handkerchief spread over Masha's face. How many of these had she brought with her, I wondered?

I sat beside Masha's body while I waited for the numbers to come in, my mind poring over the last few minutes. It had all happened so quickly. I was hit in the head, Masha was there to get me off the ground, she was shot, and then . . . and then she left me. Too quickly. A few minutes, at most.

I swallowed away the stinging in my throat and took out the icon of Saint Olga. I didn't care if it would keep me alive. Slowly, I slid it between the buttons halfway down Masha's tunic and pressed it against her heart. Only then did I listen to the numbers, only then did I pull myself together.

Pulling yourself together when half of you is dead on the ground doesn't take very long.

18

NOW that we'd cleared the way, the men scrambled across no man's land. They moved in a wave, filling in the first two trenches. They carried their rifles on their shoulders and left their masks behind. For these men, the path was safe.

I was watching a man kick a German helmet to another man, who kicked it back, when one of the women from Avilova's platoon cried out in dismay.

"Vodka!" she shouted. I rolled around to look at her. She was crouched before a wooden crate and holding a crowbar up like a flyswatter. "I think this is vodka!"

There was one crate already open, but there were at least twenty more. The Germans had left twenty crates of vodka sitting out in the open.

The men were on their way.

"Smash it!" I shouted. I ran over to her, took the crowbar, and started prying open one of the other crates. The wood strained, then the lid popped open. It, too, was full of vodka. The letters were in Latin letters, but the words looked Polish. "We have to break all the bottles!"

"But why?"

"Because if it's still here when the men get here, they'll drink it."

The girl's eyes widened, and she pulled a bottle out of the crate, smashing it against the nearest post. It shattered, catching the attention of all the other women in the trench. Lieutenant Ornilov emerged from behind a corner. His sleeve was ripped, and the skin beneath was oozing blood, but he seemed otherwise intact. I was relieved to see him still with us.

"What's going on?" he asked.

"She told us to destroy the vodka," said the first woman.

He took one look at the crates and then another at the men approaching us from the field, and his back straightened. "Do it quickly."

He took the crowbar from me and expertly ripped open several crates in the time it had taken me to do one. I smashed the bottles one by one.

"It'd be quicker if we just threw a grenade at them," I muttered.

Lieutenant Ornilov snorted and shook his head. "Someone will get hurt."

"But this is taking too long."

A moment later the trench was full of men, shoving us aside. Lieutenant Ornilov yelled at them to leave the vodka alone, but no one listened and there were too many for him to overcome, even with his pistol.

He joined me against the wall with the other woman. "This was planned," he said grimly. "The Germans left the alcohol behind just for this purpose."

The men had come at last, but they weren't enough to help keep our position, and it wasn't long before many of them were drunk.

Dismayed, we moved back to the rest of the women, and somehow, I collected my platoon. As we waited to make our next move, all I managed to accomplish was checking to see that my rifle was loaded and my bag full of grenades. The rest of the time, I sat by Masha. My fingers itched to take the icon back, but a hollow voice in the back of my mind told me it was worthless. A saint would be no help to me here.

A blast from the forest shook us in the trench. No one was hurt, but the impact pushed me against Masha's body and something poked into my thigh. I gasped from the sudden sharp pain and then pulled back to inspect the area. I didn't want to touch her because the chill of her skin made me shiver, but I did it anyway. It was traitorous to avoid her, even now, I told myself. I pulled at her waistband and lifted her up to see if there were any shards of glass beneath her, but I found nothing. Then, when I straightened her legs out again, something protruded from her empty grenade bag. It was her grandmother's hairpin.

In a trench devoid of any color but olive green, dark earth, and the whole spectrum of blood from fresh to dried, the azure glass tip shone in outright defiance. I held it close and felt myself falling into its depths, diving into a sea so blue, so clear, so quiet.

Someone shook my shoulder and I blinked. "Pavlova, wake up." It was Bochkareva. She frowned at the hairpin and I quickly stuck it into the weave of my tunic, right above my belt. "Take your platoon and clear out the woods. If you see any of the enemy, take them prisoner."

Entering the woods meant emerging from the trench, and

as much as I hated it here, the thought of going up above felt like leaping off a cliff.

"Did you get hit in the head?" she snapped. My ears were still ringing from the grenades, but I could hear her so I shook my head. "Then go! We can't give the enemy a chance to recover. We must keep moving forward."

"How long do we stay in the woods?"

She looked at me like I'd turned into a songbird. "You stay until I give you new orders. At least until dawn. As soon as I can arrange it, I'll join you." She ducked her head closer to mine and said, almost too low for me to hear it, "I have to get word back to the Tenth Army. We need at least a hundred more men."

"Why?"

She kicked at one of the broken vodka bottles. "Because there will be a counterattack. Soon. But if you clear out the nearby woods, it will delay them."

I gathered my soldiers. We double-checked our magazines of ammunition, checked one another's masks, and whispered quick prayers. A few of the women looked like rabbits preparing to leap out into a field shadowed by hawks. I smacked them on the back like Bochkareva would, hoping to steady their nerves. I didn't let my face contort to show my fear, and then I climbed up the ladder.

All fifty-two of us made it to the trees. No shots, no rattling of machine guns, not even a shout of warning. The tree trunks were riddled with bullet holes. I pressed my palm against a birch where the bark has been torn completely off, and for a split second, imagined that I knew just how the tree was feeling.

"Pavlova!" The shout came from ten meters away to my left, and I ran toward it. Korlova and Yablokova were pointing their

217

rifles into a thicket, the bayonets parting the thin brambles.

Yablokova didn't waver when she spoke. "There's a man in there. Alive."

"Toss your weapons to the side!" I shouted into the thicket. There was a rustling sound, but nothing else happened.

"Maybe he doesn't know Russian," Korlova said.

"No, but he'll understand this." I stepped forward and stabbed at the thicket.

A man crawled back on his hands and legs like a crab, but I still couldn't see him clearly through the branches and leaves. "Get. Up."

He said something in German, a sound like eggs cracking against pavement. A rifle skidded out of the thicket across the dirt, and then he raised both hands. I motioned to the others to go to him, and they each skirted the thicket, keeping their rifles trained on his chest.

Slowly, he stood, ducking his head like a penitent child. All three of us knew the instant he realized he'd been captured by women. His eyes widened, followed by a snap-quick flush of red to his cheeks as he stared at my chest. I hoisted my rifle higher.

Judging by his lack of any beard at all, he was young, but his eyes had the same haunting look Maxim's had, so he wasn't new to the horrors of this war. He said something in German again—trying to tell me his name, I realized.

"Shut it!" I didn't want to learn his name. I spat at his feet.

Korlova tied his wrists together and we brought him to a small clearing not far from the battlefield. I had them set him down by a tree stump, and then had Korlova guard him.

We captured two more of the enemy in similar fashion. I couldn't tell if they had hidden themselves during the fight and were outright cowardly pigs, or if they'd been left behind on purpose, like the vodka.

The rest of the afternoon was spent gathering all ammunition the Germans had left behind and looking for food. We managed to find a few sausages wrapped in greasy linen, and we didn't share any of it with the prisoners, despite their obvious protestations.

As night was falling and I was assigning watch, Bochkareva and the First Platoon arrived. Avilova's arm was in a sling, but she was fit enough to keep going. When I showed Bochkareva our prisoners, she almost smiled. After a day of death, the sight of her twinkling eyes in the dusk was better than extravagant praise. I shifted on my feet.

"You didn't think we'd be able to catch them?" I asked.

"I didn't think you'd be able to keep yourself from killing them."

They were fortunate at that, now that I thought about it. "Did you reach the Colonel? Is he sending reinforcements?"

"We are on our own."

Neither of us said anything for a minute. The reality that we'd been abandoned hung between us like a raven, poking at our nerves with its long beak, slashing at all veins of hope.

I needed to pull myself together. I knew I should check on my platoon, make sure everyone who'd been wounded was being treated, hand out words of encouragement to get us through the night, but all I could think about was Masha. Her warm, long fingers grown calloused, and how she was so proud of it. It marked her as one of the brave. I thought about her parents, and how whenever I'd eaten with them they'd brought me into their ongoing discussion about Russian poetry versus French, and how Masha always argued against me, even if she secretly agreed. I thought of the peony hat she bought in April, so proud to have something beautiful to wear with her grandmother's pin.

The loss of her was like acid, going down my throat one drop at a time till my whole chest burned and my lungs were too tight to inflate. When I tried to breathe, it was ragged and choking, so I gave up and let the air come into me on its own. My lungs tugged at my ribs, and somehow, I was still alive.

That was what I didn't understand. My platoon ran across no man's land. We attacked the Germans. We donned gas masks and ran through poison. We stabbed, sliced, and shot our way into these three trenches and somehow only three of us were dead. Three. And as difficult as it was to understand that Masha had fallen, it was unbelievable that I had not. I was right beside her when she was shot and yet I hadn't been hit by a single bullet.

I was scraped and bruised, and my skin itched where it came into contact with the gas. My army tunic was stained with blood—no way to tell if it was German or Russian. But I was otherwise unharmed. On the outside.

How did the machine gun miss me?

I was staring at the trees, at the scorch marks on the bone-white trunks, wondering all of this when Bochkareva punched me hard in the upper arm. Her face appeared between the trees and me, and her smile was gone.

"Save it for tomorrow, Pavlova."

"Save what?" I rubbed at my arm, amazed at how much a simple punch could hurt when the rest of me was numb.

"Your broken heart. When we get back to camp, you can stare off into space all you want, but right now, you need to be a soldier. Don't turn into a schoolgirl now. It's too late for that." She adjusted her belt, tugging her tunic down because it'd ridden up and bunched over her pistol harness. "Make sure your platoon stays alert. They're sure to attack at dawn, if not before."

I saluted and started to head toward the copse of trees Alsu had taken for our platoon, but Bochkareva stopped me by squeezing my arm, right where she'd punched me. I winced. "I know what you're feeling. I've been through it before. I can't say it will ever go away completely, but it does get better. It will for you, at least. You're a survivor. It's why I chose you as platoon leader."

She must have seen something in my face, because she shook her head and that smile was back. "No, not because of who your father is. You know I don't give a dog's tail about that. My platoon leaders are survivors. All four of you are the sort to keep your heads on in battle and come out on the other side. Like me."

She released me and marched off between the others, heading toward a cooking fire someone had set up.

I was halfway to Alsu when I realized that I could breathe deeply again. Bochkareva's words had affected me.

For so long, I'd worried that I'd prove to be gutless in the face of real danger, that I'd crumble when I most needed to steel my nerves. But I hadn't. I hadn't even thought to run away or cower.

But none of it mattered, either way, because bravery couldn't keep my best friend alive.

19

JULY 10, 1917

THE attack came shortly after midnight. The first of them.

Combined with the men—many of them barely sober enough to pick up their guns and take aim—we managed to hold our ground, and there was a pause for half an hour. The silence was broken only by the moans of the wounded, who'd been told to shut up by at least three different people. Including me.

It wasn't that I didn't have sympathy for them. I just couldn't stand the sound, knowing there was nothing anyone could do for their pain. Short of dying, they would have to wait until we got to the nurses.

We endured three more attacks, each one stronger than the last, before the Germans broke through our first line. Pointed helmets glinted in the moonlight like an iron fence weaving through the trees. I drew a grenade from my bag, pulled the pin and launched it at the first line of soldiers. They shouted and tried to jump out of the way, but my aim was as true as ever. I knocked down five in a burst of splintering wood. The women of my platoon spread around me, taking positions behind whatever solid piece of machinery or fallen log they could find. The cover was scarce, and most of us were left standing in the open.

"Take them as they come out!" I shouted while I fumbled with my magazine. It was jammed, probably because I'd rammed it in so hard during the last battle.

Pop! Pop! The sharp cutting sound of a rifle shot pierced through the ringing in my ears. It was coming from the women. Frustrated with my rifle and tempted to toss it down, I paused with the bolt still open and threw another grenade. Muravyeva was to my right, pulling off her bag of grenades and handing them to me.

"You can still stab with it," she grunted, meaning my rifle.

I was tying on her grenade bag when I heard screaming down the line. Two German infantrymen were dragging one of my soldiers into the trees. She was kicking hard, so she couldn't be severely wounded, but I couldn't tell who it was. One of mine, though.

I told Muravyeva to watch the line and then went after the men and my soldier. Crouching, I stepped over the prone bodies of my platoon, all of them ready and aimed in case someone should come from the trees.

Something in the back of my mind told me this was too dangerous. The soldier was gone, and going after her would only result in my death, too. Or worse, capture. I fingered the capsule hanging around my neck, then dropped my hand and used it to keep my balance over the earth.

Her screaming hadn't stopped. My stomach lurched while my mind raced with every possible thing they could be doing to her. I followed the sound to a little hollow surrounded by thick trees. There were just the two men, kneeling on the ground.

Their captive was still kicking and twisting, but the men were holding her down by her shoulders and knees.

I circled around the trees until their backs were to me. I was exposing my own back to the rest of their army, but there wasn't any other option. The sounds of the battle were muffled, penetrated by the occasional shell explosion. While I tried to get my bearings, the horror of the war drew away like the tide, pulling the sounds and smells away from us. And yet, this was what humanity had become: two men dragging a woman into the woods while she screamed and kicked.

She turned over and I caught a glimpse of her face. It was Alsu. Her cap lay crumpled on the ground, trodden by the men as they tried to wrestle her.

She reached for her capsule, but one of the men caught her wrist. Strangely, no one was talking. She screamed, but she didn't say anything, and the Germans had resorted to grunting and gesticulating like cavemen.

If I waited any longer, they'd have her trousers down, so with one shaky breath, I stepped forward and stabbed the first man in the back with my bayonet. It went through his ribs and, hopefully, right through his heart. The other man looked up in surprise, but I kicked him in the chin, hard. When he stumbled back, I pulled the bayonet out of the first man and lunged at him, but he was quick and managed to roll onto his knees. He scrambled to the side and grabbed Alsu. He'd gotten a knife out and held it against her neck. Her eyes bulged.

If I went after him with my bayonet, he'd slice her throat. I avoided Alsu's eyes and stared instead into his. They were dark, furious. I've killed his comrade. I could tell he was thinking about that because his eyes flicked over to the fallen man.

Slowly, I reached into my bag and wrapped my fingers

around a pin. Once I pulled it, I'd only have three to four seconds to get it in the right spot.

"Alsu, don't move," I said.

"*Du blutige Sau!*" he shouted. Harsh and crackling, his accent took on every stab of pain I'd felt over the past twenty-four hours.

There was just enough space behind him to make this work. Slowly, I slid out the pin, grateful I knew every millimeter of this weapon like it was a part of my own body. Then, still holding the level down, I pulled it up and out.

His jaw slackened, but he didn't drop the knife from Alsu's neck. He barked something that probably meant if I planned to use that, we'd all die. But he was wrong. I knew this weapon. I knew precisely how large of a blast radius it had, and I was good at throwing it.

I raised my arm and let the lever pop up.

One.

Two.

I threw it.

Three and BOOM! A fountain of dirt exploded behind them. The man flew into Alsu, and the two of them fell. I, too, stumbled backwards, but I caught my balance, choking on the dusty air. I couldn't wait long because any of his comrades could come running this direction.

I bent over them. The man's back was shredded, impaled by dozens of metal shards, a collage of muddy blood and torn uniform, pink skin and bright, white bones. Dead.

Alsu whimpered as I pulled the man off of her. She crawled onto her knees and staggered to her feet, wiping dirt from her eyes and pale cheeks. She took one glimpse at the man and shuddered.

I didn't say anything. I just took her hand and pulled her after me. We ran, death and the enemy at our heels.

We emerged into our platoon's clearing to find that our comrades were gone.

In their place were nearly a hundred Germans. They looked up, surprise and alarm written across their faces. Before they had a chance to react, we turned and ran back through the woods, weaving between the trees until we reached the edge of the forest. Ahead, our soldiers were fleeing.

"Retreat!" The call came from everywhere. It was in the vodka-soaked blood of every man I saw stumbling into and out of the trenches.

"Come on," I said to Alsu. She nodded at me, determined as always.

Together, we ran at the first trench. It was narrow, and I leaped across easily. Behind us, the enemy shot their rifles and yelled, jubilant. They followed us, but only as far as the first trench. Alsu and I raced across the field, stumbling over the bodies from the day before. The enemy had gotten their artillery back, and the proof of it raced over our heads and pounded the fields. Dirt sprayed like geysers, and ahead of me three men fell.

Pop! Pop! A bullet whizzed past me, and I risked a look over my shoulder. Not all the Germans had stopped at the trench. Four of them were running at it from the side, their greatcoats flapping in the dawn light. We'd been flanked! They were nearly upon us.

Then, as if time stopped, one of them paused, raised his rifle, and aimed at me. In that moment, I saw the way his dirty fingers gripped the trigger. There was a hint of light on the fingerboard of his rifle, a beam of sunlight that had broken over the forest. I turned away, picked up my pace . . .

Time raced forward like a train, slamming into my back. I flew forward and my whole body erupted into burning, sharp pain.

The ground hit me in the face.

I couldn't move, but I was breathing heavily and tiny grains of dirt kept rolling into my mouth, then out again.

There was a bright, screaming light, and then everything was gone.

20

JULY 10, 1917

THERE was no gradual awakening. One moment I was deep in darkness and the next I was in a hospital tent, my chest aching to breathe, daylight gushing through the open tent-flap, and my ears full of a chorus of moans, cries, and pockets of heavy silence.

I joined those who moaned for a moment, then clamped down on the weakness. My back radiated with a throbbing pain so intense the rest of my body seized up to protect it. I tried to drag a hand up to cover my eyes from the bright light, but that movement made the pain worse. I would have to accept the light, for the moment.

One cot lay between mine and the tent's canvas door. It was covered in a stack of blankets and black cases. On the cot to my right lay Muravyeva. She looked more asleep than dead and, as far as I could see, did not have any obvious wounds. Beyond her, the large tent was full of the wounded, both men and women. Nurses weaved among the cots with their trays and glass bottles. My memory of Maxim's hospital stay in Petrograd overlaid this vision, merging the two, and for a moment I had to squeeze my eyes shut.

"Private Pavlova?" a woman asked from the foot of my cot. After another blink, she came into focus—a field nurse with a long, honey-blonde braid draped over a shoulder.

"Yes."

"You're in the infirmary."

It felt like a lifetime since I'd seen a woman with such long hair, and I couldn't take my eyes off of it, remembering how Masha had saved hers for her mother. It would be with her kit still, in the barracks.

"You were shot in the back, just below your ribs," she continued, pulling me back to the moment. "The surgeon was able to get it out, and it looks like you'll make a full recovery."

I had been running across that field, between the second and third German trenches. I hadn't even made it to no-man's-land yet. Alsu was beside me—

"Where's Private Almas?"

The nurse had been holding a chart, and ran her eyes down it. "I don't have anyone here by that name. She must not have been wounded as badly as you."

"Is she alive?"

With a frown, she nodded. "I believe so. They told us the names of your dead, and I don't recognize that one."

I was about to ask her what day it was, but suddenly it didn't matter. Masha was still down there beside broken vodka bottles. Her life, extinguished for an advance that had failed.

Our first goal had been to encourage the men to fight.

Why hadn't they come to help? I didn't believe the men were cowards. Some of them had seen years of battle.

"The women in your battalion amaze me," the nurse said. "You're so brave."

I rolled my ankle because it was the only thing I could do that didn't hurt my back. "My friend is—she's dead." I swallowed, and my throat stung. "Do you know what they do? Has she been brought here?"

"A team was sent out last night to gather the dead. You must not think about that now. Rest. Do you need anything to calm your nerves?"

I shook my head, and the nurse continued to the next patient, her walk somehow both light-footed and solemn. I watched her make her way down the row of cots, mesmerized by the sway of her braid. She'd tied it with a red ribbon.

Gingerly, I pulled my arm up and brushed at my scalp. My hair had grown as long as my fingertip, and it was damp. Someone had recently washed it.

"Ekaterina."

A man stood silhouetted in the tent's bright entrance, his face too dark to see clearly, but I would know my father's shape anywhere. He came closer, moving stiffly, until he was an arm's distance from me. Too far away to touch.

"They told me you'd wake soon." His fingers brushed over the edge of my blanket. "Are you in a lot of pain?"

"I was shot."

"Yes." He looked almost embarrassed that he'd asked.

"Masha died," I said.

"Yes, I've heard. I've arranged for her body to be sent home." He reached into his pocket and pulled out the tiny icon of Saint Olga. He held it in the light for a moment and then set it on my knee, awkwardly but gently. "They say she died honorably."

"She died protecting me, sir."

"Katyusha." His voice cracked. "When they brought you

off the field, I thought . . . I wasn't sure. You—you shouldn't have come here. You shouldn't have played this game. You're my *daughter*."

"I took my platoon over three trenches. I killed men, I lost my best friend, and I was shot. This was *never* a game."

"No."

For a long time, he didn't speak, and I avoided his eyes. Talking back to him had sent a rush through my veins, which made my body ache. With a silent moan, I tried to settle back into the cot.

"It isn't a game. My apologies." He had never been so quick to apologize.

I wasn't finished. "You wanted me to be a boy, and for that, I will always be sorry."

"Don't be—"

"*I'm not sorry I'm a woman*. I'm sorry you wanted me to be a boy."

To anyone else, it would have looked as though he'd relaxed, but I knew what that slight sinking of shoulders meant. "I didn't want you to be a boy. You're a lot like your mother—no, let me finish—she was headstrong. She knew what she wanted, and she went after it. It kept me on my toes. It was the thing I loved most about her. It was also something I couldn't control. By trying to make her do what I thought was right, I drove her away."

"Papa," I whispered.

"I don't want you to be ashamed of her. Did you know, I've made sure she is comfortable? All these years I've been sending her an allowance. Even now, with the money on hold by the government . . ."

"Where is she? Is that where Maxim went?"

He skirted my questions. "She never writes. But I couldn't give up on her. I couldn't keep punishing her for being who she is. When I say you're like her, I mean it as a compliment. You have your mother's passion and you used it to do something remarkable, Katya. You are everything I could ever ask for in a child. And in a soldier."

He rested his hand on my lower leg. It was heavy but gentle. Then he was gone, marching out into the daylight and leaving my mind spinning with questions.

I spent the rest of the day slipping in and out of painful consciousness. At some point while I was asleep, Bochkareva came by with orders for me to return home with the other wounded, and Alsu hobbled in on crutches to bring me a bouquet of golden chamomile.

In the evening, when I was awake again, Lieutenant Sarkovsky came to visit, bringing me a rose blossom he'd found in the ruins of a farmhouse.

"You survived," I said to him.

He handed me the rose, then winced when its thorns snagged on my wrappings. "Sorry," he said. "Yes, I fared better than you, it looks like. We don't charge across the field like infantry soldiers, but we get shelled quite a bit. I only had a bit of a shrapnel problem."

His fingernails looked recently scrubbed, and his cuffs told the story of a dip in water. He had cleaned up for me.

"Why have you come to visit me?"

"I told you the first time we spoke: I'd heard a lot about you. I guess I feel like I know you, a little."

His eyes were kind, and so I told him. "I can't think of anyone like that, right now. I mean—"

"I know what you mean. I'm not here for that. For now,

do you want to hear a fascinating mystery story?" He held up a well-worn book. "It's quite good, even if the author isn't Russian."

I relaxed into my pillow. His voice was rather nice to hear. "All right."

The lieutenant stayed for two chapters, but my father did not return.

21

JULY 28, 1917

THE Saturday market filled the square, bursting with colors, smells, and sounds I had almost forgotten existed. I was freshly out of the hospital on my first hour of leave from the battalion, and it felt like everyone in the city had come to goggle over all the odds and ends that couldn't be found at the grocer or shops along Nevsky Prospekt.

A woman selling kielbasa smacked the hands of a little boy who'd reached out at her cart, and I jumped involuntarily. Her quick, violent movement and the boy's yelp had startled me. Both of them looked up at me.

The woman surveyed my uniform with a smirk, but the boy ran up to me, skidding to a stop before he collided with my knees.

He pointed at the Battalion of Death skull embroidered on my shoulders. "Why do you have the face of the devil up there? Are you a bad man?"

"It's a soldier, Misha," the kielbasa woman said. "And can't you see it's a woman?"

The boy squinted. "No. He has his hair cut."

I bent down, conscious that this was the first child I'd

spoken to in months. "The skull is to scare the enemy. And you know what?"

"What?"

"It worked." I stood back up, feeling better now that I'd spoken with the boy. His face was round and smooth, free of any shadows or pain. His mother had done well by him, so far.

"Then why did you jump when Mama slapped me? You shouldn't be afraid of anything."

He was right, but I didn't know how to explain to a child of four that my nerves were as shattered as a tree struck by lightning. "It just surprised me. Tell me, are you a brave boy?" He nodded. "But when you hear a bang, does it startle you?" He nodded again. "It doesn't mean you're afraid. Just that you weren't ready for the noise."

He gave me a sharp salute, which I returned before crossing the square. As I left, I heard him say, "It *was* a girl, Mama. Didn't you hear her voice?"

All around me, the city pulsed and breathed as it always had. Other children chased after the pigeons, the old bookseller leaned against his kiosk with his nose in a magazine he didn't sell, and the even older man stood on the corner, watching it all with the eyes of a crow, holding a greasy cup of black tea. As if nothing had changed while I was gone.

The city kept on, its people laughing and crying, haggling over a pair of knitted socks even though their Tsar had been removed from power and the future was about as clear as the brackish waters of the Neva.

The gruesome nature of war had not weakened Petrograd's heartbeat. Part of me wanted to scream out into the market, to tell people to take more notice. Didn't they know there were people dying for them every day?

But there was another part of me that took my heart in its hand and, with a gentle squeeze, said this was how it should be. That child by the kielbasa should never know what I had seen. Only a fellow battle-scarred soldier could share my pain.

It was right that the city and the world keep turning. This was what the fighting had been for—for them, for this city that never faltered, never paused its Saturday market even in the face of revolution and war.

Papa remained at the front, ever loyal to his men, but now I wondered if he stayed partly because the city never slowed. As long as he was away, he wouldn't have to face the revolution of life. He could continue to send money to his wife, hoping she'd return. He could imagine his son still recuperating, still preparing for an honorable return to war. He could pretend I was his dutiful girl sipping tea with the army's matrons.

I understood him for this. It was tempting to lie to myself, to pretend my best friend hadn't died or that the war we fought in would preserve this sacred land. And yet I couldn't help but look the world right in the face. When Papa finally did come home, I'd show him how to do it, too.

And if I ever heard from Maxim . . . well, we would have a lot to discuss.

I reached the flower seller. The clumps of bright yellow and pink, the spears of purple and green, and the soft peach-fuzz petals of an orange bloom were like a balm to my nerves.

"Buying some flowers for your girl—oh! You *are* a girl. I'm sorry, in that uniform, I just assumed." The flower seller covered her mouth, but her fingers couldn't hide her blush. On such a wrinkled woman, the flush of color was more charming than the array of roses behind her.

"It's all right." I ran my fingers along the edges of the fuzzy blossom, scanning the buckets filled with fresh-cut flowers until I spotted what I'd come for. With a shaking finger, I pointed. "I'll take twenty of those, please."

"Were you one of those women that fought a few weeks ago?"

"Yes, grandmother."

"Then you'll pay for only half."

It was what anyone would have haggled her down to, but it was nice not to have to do it. "Thank you."

I paid, waited for her to wrap the flowers, and retreated from the bustling market. I turned down a narrow alley that few would think to enter, grateful for its silence.

The cemetery was a field of fresh stones.

"You're here," Masha's mother said when I approached.

"One of my doctors at the front had me discharged," I said quietly. "He said I can re-enlist once I fully recover." *If you fully recover* was what he'd really said.

Sabina Andreyevna did not smile, but she nodded appreciatively at the bouquet in my arms. She wore a black kerchief that hung low on her brow. It hid her hair, but I knew it was just as dark, just as shiny, as Masha's own.

I didn't know what to say to the mother of my dead friend. I couldn't bear to tell her how much Masha had meant to me, that she'd died saying she wasn't afraid, or that she'd traded her life for mine.

Sabina Andreyevna knelt at the gravestone and wept without noise. "She loved you," she said.

"I know." I got on my knees beside her and laid the flowers at Masha's grave. They were the prettiest blush-pink peonies

I'd ever seen, each bloom a declaration. The moment I saw them in the market, I knew they had grown for Masha. "She had this hat," I began, but I couldn't finish.

"That silly hat," she said. "It cost her an entire month of wages. I was so irritated."

"It made her happy."

"Yes. And that was why I smiled every time she put it on."

With the tip of my finger, I traced Masha's name on the headstone, letting the granite dig into the skin.

"There's an award ceremony tomorrow morning," I said after a while. "Some of us are being given the Cross of Saint Georgi."

"Yes, I'll be there. They're giving the mothers of—of—I'll be there." What she couldn't say was that the mothers of the dead were receiving medals in their stead.

I pushed myself off my knees and stood, then tugged my uniform tunic down and readjusted my brother's belt.

"Till tomorrow, then."

After another quick glance at where Masha lay, I left her mother standing there alone, her feet blanketed with flowers.

Sub-Lieutenant Maria Bochkareva marched down the line swinging her sharp, shining sabre. She stopped in front of each of us, her expression severe but her eyes soft, and pinned a medal to each of our chests. When she reached me, I looked beyond her, through her, at the horizon, as we'd been taught to do—but also because I couldn't bear for her to see how much I did not want this.

"Private Pavlova, for bravery on the field and for daring to rescue a soldier taken by the enemy, I award you the Cross of Saint Georgi. May the gold and black ribbon declare to all your proven valor in battle." She slid the metal pin through my blouse, expertly avoiding my skin, and snapped it closed.

When she was done, she went to the front of the entire battalion and turned to face us all.

"Our sisters in battle," she said, her voice ringing across the courtyard, "those who stand among us now and those who have sacrificed themselves for Russia, will never abandon us. We have a bond that cannot be broken. And it should never be forgotten. Go! Enjoy this day with your families."

Masha's mother found me standing alone on the crushed grass of the parade ground. It seemed as though everyone else was surrounded by husbands or fathers, mothers or sisters, and I had no one. Not here.

"She would have liked all this fuss, wouldn't she?" she asked.

I snorted. "She would have pinned her medal on her newest hat." Part of me was shouting at me not to joke about Masha, but another part had to. Because to not laugh meant I had to cry, and I was dry.

"Her father wanted to be here," said Sabina Andreyevna. "But he's not strong enough yet to stand for long stretches. He's proud of you too, though. Sometimes in the night I fancy I can still hear him and Masha talking about economics, or reciting poems, or just laughing. There was so much laughter."

Then it came to me, that although Sabina Andreyevna had not been there in the battle, had not seen the nightmare I had seen, she understood what I had lost. In that, we were the same. My friend, her daughter, had left us gasping for meaning, our memories filled with the laughter and mischief of the tall girl who'd bought silk peonies in winter.

My throat constricted, and I had to turn away and bite my lip till it pinched. Then Sabina Andreyevna's arm was around my shoulders. "You should come to our house sometimes. It's too quiet there now. When you need to, you come to me."

———

The next day, I saw Alsu off at the train station; she was going home to heal. She carried everything she owned in a canvas bag slung over her shoulder. I would have offered to help her carry it, but I knew she was strong despite her wounded leg. She looked odd in her civilian clothes, and when I pointed it out, she told me I looked like a boy in his father's uniform. And we laughed.

"What did you do with your boots?" I asked, noting the absence of lumps in the bag.

She smiled all the way up to her rose-printed headscarf and lifted the hem of her skirt off the ground. "I wore them there, I wore them back, and I'm not taking them off until I get where I'm going." It was such an Alsu thing to say.

We stepped into the street and crossed over the rail of the trolley line.

"It's going to take three trains to get home," she remarked.

"That's not so bad."

"No, it isn't." I could nearly taste the bittersweet words she didn't say: *I'm lucky to be alive—the number of trains doesn't matter.*

We skirted a clump of people gathered in front of the station and found our way to the platform. While she picked up her tickets, I bought her a sweet roll wrapped in wax paper from the kiosk. And then we were just two women waiting for the train.

"What are your plans when you get home?" I asked.

She bit into the sweet roll. "I told you, remember? I'm taking my girls to Greece. That's when I'm taking off my boots. When we get to the strand and the sea."

She *had* said that, a lifetime ago. One of the nights in the barracks when we thought we'd be heroes.

"I remember. And Masha said she'd like to visit you there."

I didn't want to talk about Masha. I never would. And I always wanted to talk about her, and I always would. Alsu took my hand in hers and squeezed it. She knew.

"Did you see Muravyeva after the ceremony?" I asked. "They're sending her back to the front, to the rest of the battalion."

"Yes. She said Bochkareva made her platoon leader. It's what she wanted, and she looked very happy."

"The battalion isn't going to fight right away, though. I think they're being handed over to a reserve company."

Alsu finished her roll, watching me. "What about you? What is the brave Private Pavlova going to do now? Will she go back to the army?"

I shook my head. In truth, I hadn't decided. "I'm going to write to you," I said. "That's what I'm going do. But you have to write to me first, with your new address in Greece."

I pulled out a pen and scrap of paper from my pocket and jotted down my address. The train arrived then, all snorts of steam and wails of iron.

"I'm going to convince you to come south," she grinned. "You'll get my first letter when winter's starting to freeze the dew here." She crumpled the wax paper from her roll and tossed it into a garbage bin. The paper with my address, however, she folded in half and tucked into her little stack of train tickets.

As the train huffed away and she waved goodbye from her window seat, I knew it was the last time I'd ever see Alsu Almas. It was odd to know this. The last time I'd waved goodbye to anyone, it had been to Sergei when I was leaving for the front. The time before that it had been Maxim, at this very spot.

He should have found a safe place by now. Maybe he'd found our mother. Or maybe he'd run off to Europe, or America. I might never know.

I wanted to find Maxim and tell him that I finally understood. He needed to find peace. There are worthy wars fought badly and unworthy ones fought well, and all of them are hell. They may save nations or break them, but they always take more than they give back.

Ilya.

Masha.

And Maxim.

And yet perhaps I could still make sure this war didn't take everything.

22

JULY 31, 1917

THE Crosses was a monstrous red-brick building that squatted along the river embankment. Four wings met in the center and formed, appropriately, a giant cross. It was notorious for holding political prisoners, as well as murderers and thieves. One last time, I checked that my medal was on straight and then marched to the gates.

The prison guards eyed me curiously.

"I need to speak with the warden. I'm here to release a prisoner."

One guard, a bear of a man with a beard long gone out of fashion, snickered. "Go on inside, girl."

"I'm Private Ekaterina Pavlova."

"Private," the other one said. Surprisingly, his tone held an ounce of respect. "You can ask the warden for your man, but it's not likely they'll let you have him. Depends on what he's here for."

Clearly, they were hoping for more information, but I wasn't going to give it to them. I passed through the checkpoint and made my way inside. After that, a few strategic names and a letter from General Yudenich got me to the cell.

Before the jailer unlocked the door, I peeked in through its little window and caught a glimpse of Sergei. He was pacing, but when the door started to open, he crossed his arms and tucked his hands inside his elbows.

He was an age older. His hair was greasy, his beard had grown in uneven patches, and his sleeves were ripped at the shoulders.

"You're being released," the jailer said, and Sergei's eyes widened. Then he looked past the jailer and saw me, half in shadow and half in the light of the hallway's single burning lightbulb.

"Katya?" His eyes traveled over me, pausing at the medal in the center of my chest. He searched my face as though looking for confirmation that I was truly Katya and not some impostor. I wasn't sure I could offer the proof he sought.

I nodded crisply. "Let's go."

I didn't speak to him again until we'd signed him out and made it to the cab.

As I climbed in, my stitches pinched where my belt dug into them, and I winced.

"What is it?" Sergei asked. "Are you hurt?"

The cab driver leaned back to us. "Where to now?"

"Home," I said, gasping.

"What's wrong with her?" Sergei asked him.

"She got shot, and it hurts." The driver said it so matter-of-factly, I nearly laughed.

Sergei pulled me forward a little, tugging on my uniform and probably looking for signs of blood.

"Not today, you idiot," I managed. "I'm fine. Just need to get this belt off." He reached for my buckle and I slapped his hand away. "It can wait," I growled.

The driver slapped the reins and we rocked back into the seats, grabbing the sides of the cab.

After a moment Sergei asked, hesitantly, "How severely were you wounded?"

"It could have been worse." I wanted to tell him about Masha, but I couldn't find the words. How do you describe your friend's last breath?

"I see you've been busy while I was gone," I said to change the subject.

His jaw tightened. "I was in the wrong place at the wrong time. I'm sure they would have released me in a few more days. They 'interviewed' me again today, and I didn't have anything more to say. It wasn't so bad, except I have no idea what happened to the others, or what's been going on."

I knew how that felt. "Well, we can stop at my place— Paulina can feed you before you go home."

We rode in silence the rest of the way home. I paid the driver a small fortune and then took Sergei upstairs to my apartment. He waited in the sitting room while I found Paulina and asked her to bring in a tray.

When I rejoined him, he was busy laying out the chess board. He looked up as I entered and smiled, sheepishly. "I've been bored for weeks."

"And you choose chess to allay your boredom?" I tried to smile, but my lips just couldn't do it.

"Do you have anything to drink?"

"The cabinet was empty when I got back."

He frowned. "Your brother?"

I shook my head. Maxim would have gone for the silver, not the vodka. "I still don't know where he's gone," I said, doing my best to sound as though it didn't matter. I hoped that wherever he was, he felt less haunted now than he had when he was home.

I picked up the white knight and rolled it in my palm. When Maxim and I played chess, we had always called this knight General Pavlov, because someday that's who our father would be. The black knight always fought against the Tsar's army, usually as a leader of Turks. I handed Sergei the black knight.

A smile crept up the side of his mouth. "I knew you'd choose the white knight."

"I should repaint these. White and red," I said, picking up my knight and tapping it against his black horse.

More solemnly, he said, "Which one will you choose then?"

"Whichever side plays with the most honor."

He rolled his eyes, dissatisfied with my answer, but I couldn't give him the one he wanted. I couldn't be like him, a Bolshevik through and through—no more than I could be like my father, blindly loyal to the past. "You were wrong before," I said.

"Pardon?"

"At the train station, when I left for the front. You were wrong about the war. About Russia. And most of all, about my battalion."

"I wasn't wrong. I knew you would be brave out there." He nodded at my medal. "And clearly you were."

"But you didn't believe it would make a difference."

He eyed me cautiously. "Has it? Last time I checked, the war isn't over."

"But that's where you were wrong. We were both wrong."

"How so?"

"Thinking the end of the war would be the end of our troubles." Images of my brother, my father, my friends swam

246

at the edges of my eyes. "I'm not sure it'll ever be over. Not for me. I don't think any government, any reform, any victory can make things right." I stared down at the knight in my hand. "But I know now that I won't run from whatever comes next."

We continued setting up the board and in my mind each pawn became a soldier I knew. Masha and Alsu were my knights, Ilya a bishop, Maxim a rook, my father the king, Bochkareva the freewheeling queen.

I gave no quarter.

AUTHOR'S NOTE

Women's history is so often hidden in the cracks of time, it's hard to envision women doing anything other than marrying, bearing children, and suffering. Unless you count the handful of queens and empresses we all know about. The history of women in war is even more obscure, since most of military history has been recorded by men who often overlook (due to accident, ignorance, or embarrassment) any female warriors. For example, anthropologists recently discovered that a Viking burial site did not, in fact, belong to a great war chieftain, but to a *chieftess*. For over a hundred years, she was assumed to be a man because of the weapons buried with her. It took DNA testing—done by a team of archaeologists led by a woman—to prove otherwise.

I did not learn about the Women's Battalion of Death during my college Russian history courses, so it was a punch to the gut when I first discovered them. Who would have joined this battalion, and why? A girl like Katya, of course.

As soon as I began researching this topic, I couldn't get enough of it. I returned to Saint Petersburg—called Petrograd during World War I—to walk the streets Katya would have walked, to visit museums that might contain relevant items or documents, and to search high and low for anything related to the Women's Battalion. The surviving information is not easily available to the public, unfortunately.

The 1st Russian Women's Battalion spawned several other women's battalions, including the 1st Petrograd Women's Battalion, which unsuccessfully defended the Winter Palace, the residence of the Tsar's family, from the Bolshevik takeover in October 1917. After the Bolsheviks, led by Vladimir Lenin, wrested power from the more moderate provisional government, all the women's battalions were officially disbanded. Some former members joined the Bolsheviks' Red Army while others joined the remnants of the Imperial White Army.

In March 1918, the Bolshevik government signed a treaty with Germany and its allies, ending Russia's involvement in World War I. Maria Bochkareva hopped a ship to the United States, where she met President Wilson in person and begged him to help save Russia from the Bolsheviks. Unsuccessful in this effort, she returned to Russia and joined the Imperial Army. On May 16, 1920, she was executed by the Red Army as an "enemy of the working class" at the age of 30.

This was not the end of women's involvement in the Russian military, however. Decades later, during World War II, women served in all areas of the armed forces. The only all-female unit, a regiment of female aviators nicknamed the Night Witches, distinguished themselves by their valor.

Despite my best efforts, this novel doubtless contains some historical inconsistencies and anachronisms. All errors are entirely my own. All dates are in the Old Style/Julian Calendar, which Russia followed until 1918. The flyer that Katya and Masha receive while at the factory is a snippet from a poem posted around Novgorod in May 1917.

If you wish to learn more about Russia during this tumultuous period in time (it was tumultuous for most of the world, but I think Russia takes the cake), here are some places to begin:

Stoff, Laurie S. *They Fought for the Motherland: Russia's Women Soldiers in World War I and the Revolution.*

Bochkareva, Mariia. Yashka, *My life as Peasant, Exile, and Soldier.*

Marxists Internet Archive, Marxists.org.

Pipes, Richard. *A Concise History of the Russian Revolution.*

Reed, John. *Ten Days that Shook the World.*

Stone, Norman. *The Eastern Front.*

TOPICS FOR DISCUSSION

1. Why is Katya working in the munitions factory? What values drive her choices?

2. Katya is torn between her father's loyalty to the authoritarian Tsar and the radical new ideas of the socialists. What problems does she see with each side?

3. How has Maxim's experience in the army affected him? What aspects of his inner turmoil is Katya missing?

4. Why is Sergei upset that Katya is thinking of joining the Women's Battalion? How are his views different from—and similar to—the views expressed by Elena Stefanovna?

5. Why does Masha disapprove of the women's rights faction in the battalion?

6. What fragments of information do the women learn about Bochkareva's background? How do you think this background might affect her personality and actions?

7. Why is the story of Saint Olga important to Katya? What does it remind her of? Why does it inspire her?

8. Katya, Masha, Alsu, and Avilova all have different reasons for joining the battalion. Which character's motivations do you find most relatable and why?

9. Reread the scene in which Katya and the other women try to prevent the men from getting to the vodka left by the Germans. When the men find and drink it all anyway, how do you think this makes Katya feel? What does this single moment tell her about the Women's Battalion's overall mission?

10. What does Katya's conversation with her father in the infirmary reveal about him? How do you think this might change their relationship in the future?

11. When Katya is home from the front, mourning Masha, what do the orange flowers and the memory of Masha's hat symbolize for her?

12. Katya says, "There are worthy wars fought badly and unworthy ones fought well, and all of them are hell." Consider another famous conflict. How do you think it compares to Katya's experience of World War I? Do you think it was "worthy" or "unworthy," and what is the difference?

13. What, if anything, do you think the women's sacrifices have accomplished—for their country or for themselves?

14. By the end of the novel, how have Katya's motivations shifted? Where do her loyalties lie now?

ACKNOWLEDGMENTS

Historical novels cannot be written alone, and *Open Fire* is no exception. I owe thanks to my Russian history and language teachers from twenty years ago as much as I do to contemporary professors and researchers who wrote about Russia in 1917.

Thanks goes first and foremost to the women soldiers of Russia. They were my inspiration and have become my heroes. Without these women paving the way in both World Wars, I might not have been able to join the military in the late 20th century. Yes, they were from another country, but the news traveled far and wide.

I am indebted to Dr. Laura S. Stoff for writing such a comprehensive and engaging study about Russian female soldiers in World War I. It was the book I reached for most often.

A thousand thanks to my comrade Elizabeth Wein, who walked the snowy streets of Saint Petersburg and Moscow with me. You are the best book-research traveling companion a writer can have. I will split another Soviet champagne with you any day of the week.

Thanks also goes to the Parks Guard Rifle Drill Team at Saint Louis University, where I made my first "battle" friends and learned how to clean a rifle that had been purposely stuffed full of sticks and mud. 1903-A3s for the win!

Большое спасибо to my Russian professors, Yelena Ivanovna Belyaeva-Standen and Dr. David Murphy, and to the world's best Russian history professor, Dr. Dan Schlafly. You taught me to love Russia, past and present. Thanks to my friend Val Afanasyev, who sent me an icon of Saint George when I was in Iraq, and who took me to the World War I Museum in Saint Petersburg many years later.

Many thanks to my writer friends who all contributed in one way or another, near and far: Laurie Halse Anderson, MJ Auch, Suzanne Bloom, Maya Chhabra, Bruce Coville, Charlotte Coville, P.M. Freestone, Emma Kress, JP McCormack, Laura Lam, Natalie C. Parker, and Ellen Yeomans. And the Writers Without Borders—thank you for always listening.

This book would have gone nowhere if it weren't for my agent, Laura Rennert, who made sure I wrote the right story.

To Amy Fitzgerald, Supreme Editor and fellow Russophile, who truly understood Katya's story—спасибо, моя подруга.

To my parents and sister, who have always been there and challenged me mentally, thank you. Elizabeth and Henry, thank you for being the most understanding of children. Also, it's okay if you never read this.

And finally, to Jim: you always have my back, and I've got yours.

ABOUT THE AUTHOR

Amber Lough is an Air Force veteran and world traveler. She loves fountain pens, the great outdoors, foreign languages, and cats. Amber lives in Germany with her husband and their two children. She is also the author of the YA fantasy novels *The Fire Wish* and *The Blind Wish*.